# THE PET SHOW
# MYSTERY

# TRIXIE BELDEN.

# The TRIXIE BELDEN Series

# TRIXIE BELDEN®

# THE PET SHOW MYSTERY

**By Kathryn Kenny**
**Black-and-white illustrations by Jim Spence**

**A GOLDEN BOOK • NEW YORK**

**Western Publishing Company, Inc., Racine, Wisconsin 53404**

# Contents

# 1 * An Everlasting Winter

"I CAN'T STAND IT," Trixie Belden proclaimed as she came in through the back door of her family's comfortable old farmhouse. "I absolutely can't stand it one more minute."

Trixie's mother looked up from her work in the kitchen, an expression of gentle concern on her face. "What's wrong, Trixie?" she asked.

"Winter. School. Snow. *Home*work. *Boredom*." Trixie made each word a longer, louder groan.

"Why, Trixie!" Helen Belden said. "Today

was your first day back at school after two weeks' winter vacation. How can you be bored with it already?"

Trixie sighed as she unzipped her down-filled jacket. She hung it and her book bag on a hook and walked into the kitchen. "I don't know why I'm bored, but I am. Maybe it really isn't school I'm tired of; maybe it's this awful, everlasting *winter*."

"It has been a hard one," her mother agreed.

"Hard? It's been impossible!" Trixie exclaimed as she opened the refrigerator door in search of an after-school snack. "First we had that enormous snowstorm two days before Thanksgiving. Then we had another one three days *after* Thanksgiving. Things never really got dug out between the two storms. And then, right after the second one, it turned bitterly cold for two entire weeks. Everything froze solid so it *couldn't* be dug out. And that's how it's been ever since.

"The cold and snow make it impossible to go anywhere or do anything," Trixie went on. "I'm glad they added a second run of the school bus every day so country kids like us could still take part in activities after school. Still, that only gives us an extra hour and a half. The rest of the time, we're cooped up at home without one single, solitary thing to do," she concluded as she set the food down on the counter.

"I think you're exaggerating," her mother said. "What you mean is that the Bob-Whites' usual whirlwind of activity has been slowed to a stiff breeze."

In spite of her bad mood, Trixie had to smile. The Bob-Whites of the Glen—a group that included Trixie and her two older brothers, plus their four best friends—were indeed an active group.

The club's two purposes were to have fun and to help others. And no matter what else they did, they seemed to stumble accidentally onto mysteries that needed to be solved. At least, Trixie insisted that the Bob-Whites got involved in the mysteries by accident. Her friends thought that Trixie went out of her way to find them. She readily admitted that she enjoyed the excitement.

"Excitement," she said out loud as she sliced apples and pears and cheese and arranged the slices on a plate. "That's what we need around here."

"Speak for yourself," Mrs. Belden said. "After all the excitement of the holidays, I don't mind having a couple of quiet weeks."

"The quiet weeks go on for *months*," Trixie said, unwilling to look at the bright side of anything. "That's the problem."

Just then the back door opened again, and a heavily bundled figure stepped inside. "I've found the solution to all of our problems," he announced. "Cybernetics."

Trixie and her mother looked at one another, startled by the perfect timing of the remark. Both of them began to giggle.

"I fail to see the humor in my statement." Mart Belden's frowning face emerged as he took off his stocking cap and unzipped his jacket.

Trixie didn't need to see her brother's sandy hair, blue eyes, and freckles—all so much like her own—to be able to identify him. Mart was the only member of the Belden household who used such pompous language.

"Never mind," Trixie said quickly. "Anyway, tell me about this cider-whoosits and how it's going to solve all our problems."

"Cy-ber-net-ics," Mart repeated slowly. "Electronic communication control systems. Computers, to the uninitiated."

"That's right, you're taking a computer programming class this term," Mrs. Belden said. "I see you're enjoying it so far."

"Enjoyment is only part of it. *Enrichment* is the central concern," Mart said loftily. "Today I had my first hands-on experience with state-of-the-art technology. Already I can feel the parameters of my personal data base expanding in quantum leaps."

"I can't stand it," Trixie said. "I really can't stand it."

As Trixie spoke, the back door opened a third time and Brian Belden stepped inside. His nose and the tips of his ears were bright red, and his dark eyes were sparkling with amusement. "Let me guess. Mart was telling you about his vast experience with computers—all twenty minutes of it."

"Why, how did you know?" Trixie asked her oldest brother in mock amazement.

"Easy," Brian said. "He talked about nothing else all the way home. I almost wished I'd ridden the bus, instead of taking my car so we could run an errand after school."

"Obviously, neither of you has envisioned the possibilities," said Mart. "I can learn to use an electronic spreadsheet, for example.

Then I'll be a more effective treasurer for the Bob-Whites. I'll be able to trace our transactions, do quarterly financial analyses, produce long-term projections—"

"You're going to do all those things?" Trixie asked. "The Bob-White treasury hardly ever has more than five dollars in it. That wouldn't be worth the money you'd need to run the computer!"

"You haven't grasped the intricacies of control theory," Mart sniffed. He gathered up as much fruit and cheese as he could carry in one hand and picked up his book bag with the other. "I can't spend more time trying to explain it; I have work to do."

"I do, too," Brian said. "Of course, I don't have any interesting classes—just boring old science, math, history, and English lit. But I'll apply myself to my studies as best I can." Scooping his books up off the counter where he'd set them, he followed his brother up the stairs.

The bantering exchange with her brothers had almost made Trixie forget about her boredom. But as soon as they left the room, all of her energy seemed to go with them. "I should study, too, I guess," she said, but she didn't make any move toward her book bag. Impulsively, she asked, "Moms, can I go over to the Manor House to see Honey?"

"But you just rode home together on the school bus," Mrs. Belden said.

"I know, but we can't *talk* on the bus. It's so crowded and noisy. Seeing Honey will cheer me up. Please? I'll be back by dinner time, I promise."

"All right," Mrs. Belden said. "It sounds to me like a good winter tonic."

"The best!" Trixie agreed. She dashed for the back door, and pulled on her boots and jacket. Calling good-bye, she headed outdoors.

The cold stabbed at her like an icy knife. Walking down the long driveway of Crabapple Farm required her to face the wind, and her eyes watered and her forehead ached. *Maybe this wasn't such a great idea after all*, she thought. *Especially since the path between our house and the Wheelers' is snowed over. Going down Glen Road is almost twice as far*.

At Glen Road, she turned and began walking toward the Manor House. The wind shifted, and she was still walking directly into it. She walked with her head down, her eyes watching her boots as she trudged through the snow.

When she looked up again, she saw something dark at the side of the road several yards ahead. She blinked away the tears that blurred her vision. The thing wasn't a bush, because its outline was too distinct for that. It wasn't a cluster of rural mailboxes, either—there weren't any between the Manor House and Crabapple Farm.

Finally Trixie began to make sense of the strange shape. *It's some kind of four-legged animal*, she thought. *No—wait. It's a person on hands and knees. But why would a person be kneeling in the snow by the side of the road?*

"Oh, no!" she shouted. "It must have been a hit-and-run accident!" She began to run as fast as she could in her bulky clothes toward the person.

As Trixie drew near, the person began to rise, slowly and awkwardly. *You should never get up if you're hurt*, Trixie thought frantically, recalling her first-aid training.

She sprinted the last few feet and then lunged forward, reaching out. "Let me help you!" she called.

Startled by the sound of Trixie's voice, the person whirled around, colliding with Trixie's outstretched arms. Something was knocked to the ground and landed on the hard snow with a soft thud. At the same time, hundreds of small golden pellets flew up into the air.

"What do you think you're doing?" a girl's voice asked. She was dressed in heavy pants, a hooded parka, and a knit muffler.

"I-I was trying to help," Trixie stammered, surprised at meeting someone on the icy road. "Are you hurt?"

"You didn't run into me that hard," the girl said. "I just dropped my corn, is all."

"No, I mean before. I saw you on your hands and knees, and I thought you were hurt," Trixie explained.

"Oh." The girl paused to consider Trixie's theory. "I guess I can see why you'd think that. But I've spent plenty of time on my hands and knees along this road, and nobody else ever thought that."

"You have?" Seeing the girl's blank look, Trixie added, "Spent plenty of time kneeling out here, I mean. Why?"

"Feeding the birds. That was a bowl of cracked corn that you just knocked out of my hands."

"Sorry," Trixie said belatedly. "But why are you out here feeding the birds? We get dozens and dozens at the feeder in our backyard."

"Not these birds, you don't," the girl said. "These are birds like pheasants and quail. They feed off the ground, not from feeders. But when there's as much snow as there's been this winter, the ground is all covered. The birds can't get to their food. They're dying by the thousands."

"Oh." It was Trixie's turn to pause and consider. "It seems like I've seen more pheasants this winter than usual, though."

"You have," the girl said. "They're so desperate for food that they're coming out of the underbrush to hunt for food along the roadside."

"So that's why you're putting the corn out here," Trixie concluded, hoping that she was finally on the right track.

"I have ten feeding stations along a three-mile section of Glen Road. I have ten more along Old Telegraph Road. Every day I come out and refill one set of stations or the other. It isn't much, but it's the best I can do."

"I think what you're doing is wonderful," Trixie said sincerely. "It's been a hard winter.

Walking three miles out and three back every day takes real dedication."

"My dedication won't keep the birds alive," the girl said bitterly. "Only the food will help. And I'm not putting out nearly as much as is needed."

"But you're doing all you can," Trixie insisted. "That's all anyone can do."

The girl shrugged off Trixie's reassurances. "I know, but it just isn't enough."

There was an awkward silence. Trixie couldn't think of anything to say that wouldn't come pelting back in her face the way the cracked corn had. "My name is Trixie Belden," she said finally.

"I know who you are," the girl told her.

Trixie peered through the fur-trimmed hood and knit muffler, trying to recognize the girl. It was no use.

"My name is Norma Nelson," the girl finally said.

"Oh! Hi. Of course, I know you." Trixie realized that she was speaking with more warmth than was really appropriate. Something about Norma's sullen coldness made Trixie desperately want to produce some sign of a thaw. Actually, though, she didn't know Norma Nelson

at all. Hearing the name, Trixie could picture
the girl's face and see her walking down the
halls of Sleepyside Junior-Senior High
School. But as far as Trixie could remember,
she'd never spoken to Norma before.

"I have to get going," Norma said. "It's getting dark."

"Can I help you with the rest of your route?
It's my fault that you're behind schedule, after
all."

"I can manage." Norma Nelson picked up a
large plastic pail and a stack of smaller plastic
bowls. Without saying good-bye, she walked
off in the direction from which Trixie had just
come.

## 2 * Patch Provides a Plan

TRIXIE WATCHED Norma for a moment before turning and continuing on toward the Manor House. *I don't even know where Norma lives,* she thought. *She must live in town, or I'd have seen her on the school bus. It really takes guts to make that hike every afternoon, the way the weather's been.*

"It certainly does," Honey Wheeler agreed a few minutes later. Settled in Honey's bedroom, Trixie had immediately related her encounter with Norma Nelson. "It kind of surprises me. Norma has always seemed so quiet and timid."

"Do you know her?" Trixie asked.

Honey shook her head, and her honey-blonde hair moved softly across her shoulders. "I had an English class with her once. She never raised her hand, and when the teacher called on her, there was always a long, long pause. I sometimes had the feeling that Norma might not say anything at all. But finally she'd answer. She always knew the right answer, too. She's not dumb or anything. She's just shy."

"It's hard for me to imagine being that shy. It's never been one of my bigger problems," Trixie said, laughing at herself.

Honey didn't join in the laughter. "I can do more than imagine it. I can remember what it's like. It's no fun, believe me."

Both girls sat quietly for a moment, remembering the days when Honey Wheeler had first moved to the Manor House just down the road from Crabapple Farm. She'd been pale, shy, and frightened of her own shadow. The only child of wealthy parents who traveled much of the time, she'd been raised in boarding schools. Most of her problems had come from not having a real home, with real friends and neighbors.

Realizing that, the Wheelers had bought the Manor House with its horses, stables, and acres of game preserve. They'd also hired Miss Trask, one of Honey's teachers from boarding school, to come and manage the house full-time.

The Wheelers' plan for helping their daughter had succeeded even better than they'd hoped. The success was largely due to the bold and energetic Belden youngsters who became Honey's closest neighbors and, in short order, best friends.

To make things "perfectly perfect," as Honey was fond of saying, soon after Trixie met Honey, the two girls met Jim Frayne, a runaway orphan. After Jim had escaped from his cruel stepfather and found his rightful inheritance, he'd been adopted by the Wheelers.

In just a few months, Honey had a real home, best friends, and an older brother. "Coming to Sleepyside was like the start of a new life for me," Honey said aloud.

"It was for me, too," Trixie said. "Even with two older brothers and one younger one, I've felt lonely sometimes. Now that you're here, I never feel that way anymore."

"I'm sure it helps that my brother Jim is here, too," Honey said playfully.

Trixie grinned. There was a special friendship between Trixie and Jim, and all of the Bob-Whites knew about it. But Trixie hadn't quite been able to admit those feelings yet, not even to herself. "Maybe I did too much to help you overcome your shyness," Trixie said. "Now you tease me as badly as Brian and Mart do."

"I could *never* tease you the way Mart does," Honey countered. "I'd certainly never resort to anything so low as calling you 'Beatrix.'"

"Ugh!" Trixie cringed at the sound of her hated real name. "Well, when he does that I can always get even by calling him my 'almost twin.' He hates the fact that he's only eleven months older than I am."

"He tries so hard to act older and wiser," Honey pointed out. "From the way he talks, you'd think he was eleven *years* older."

"You should hear him now!" Trixie said. "He's taking a computer course this term, and he came home sounding like a floppy disk."

Trixie sighed and sank back against the wall. "In a way, though, I envy Mart. He has his computer class to look forward to every day. What do I have? Snow and ice and cold. Yuch!"

"I know what you mean. When we were off traveling upstate trying to find my brother, I really believed we were doing something important. There's no other feeling quite as good."

"That's it exactly!" Trixie said. "See? I knew you'd understand how I feel, even though nobody else seems to. I just can't believe there's nothing important in the world to do in winter. I think we don't have enough gumption to go out in the cold and find the things that need to be done."

"The way Norma Nelson has, you mean?" Honey asked quietly.

"Yes, the way—wait a minute! Honey, that's it! Why can't the Bob-Whites start a feeding program, too?"

"Oh, Trixie, that's a wonderful idea. We'll use what's in the treasury to buy cracked corn. We could start our route where Norma's leaves off, since we live farther out in the country."

Trixie nodded. Her thoughts were already

churning furiously. "That's not enough, though. If we start only a couple more routes, we'll wind up feeling as defeated as Norma does. We need to get lots more people involved. Imagine what would happen if everyone in Sleepyside were feeding the birds!"

"We could save nearly all of them," Honey said. "But how do we do it?"

"I don't know, but we'll think of something. I'll tell you what, you talk to Jim. I'll talk to Brian and Mart. Tomorrow at school we'll talk to Di and Dan, too." Diana Lynch and Dan Mangan were the two newest Bob-Whites. They were often busy with family chores, so the time they spent on club projects was limited. "Then we can meet back here tomorrow after dinner." Trixie rose and reached for her jacket. "I have to get home for dinner now. I'll see you on the bus tomorrow. Maybe by then I'll have an idea."

"Maybe I will, too," Honey said. "Oh, Trixie, the weather seems better already."

At dinner that night, Trixie told her family about the need to save the game birds. "Norma says they're dying by the thousands. We have to do something."

"Thousands is a lot," Trixie's six-year-old

brother Bobby said solemnly. "Can I help you save the birds, Trixie?"

"Of course you can," she promised. "We can all help. We just don't know how yet."

"Why don't you ask Norma Nelson if she has any ideas?" Brian asked. "After all, she's had the subject on her mind longer than we have. Maybe she's thought of some new approaches, but she's been too shy to ask anyone for help."

"That's a wonderful idea, Brian!" Trixie exclaimed. "I'll do it. The next time I see Norma at school, I'll talk to her about it."

When she saw Norma between classes the next morning, Trixie greeted her excitedly. "Hi, Norma," she said, stopping in the middle of the crowded hallway. "How did the rest of your route go yesterday?"

Norma looked at Trixie blankly. "Fine," she replied. Then, to Trixie's amazement, she walked right on down the hall. Even indoors, Norma walked as though she were bundled up in heavy clothing. As dozens of laughing, talking students pushed past her, she trudged along, head down, as though she were alone on Glen Road.

Trixie told the other Bob-Whites about the

incident when they were gathered that night
in the Wheelers' den. A fragrant bowl of hot
cider, spiced with cinnamon and cloves, sat
on the coffee table. Next to it was a platter
heaped with oatmeal raisin cookies.

"Can you believe it?" Trixie said. "She had
to know I was about to say something else. But
she just left me standing there. That's rude!"

"In a way, you're lucky," Mart said. "I've
reached the conclusion that it's better to be ig-
nored by an expert than hovered over by one."

"I have a feeling we aren't talking about
Norma Nelson anymore," Brian said.

Mart shook his head. "Gordon Halvorson,
from my computer class. His father is a computer programmer, and they've owned a computer since practically the first day there *was*
such a thing. Since he knows so much, I
thought he'd be a good person to help me
learn. I asked him a couple of questions, and
presto! He's my personal instructor, at my side
every minute."

"Isn't that good?" Di Lynch asked. "I'm
sure I'd need lots of help in a class like that."

"But he isn't helpful," Mart said. "He's just
bossy. He practically tells me every key to

push before I have time to figure it out for myself. That's no way to learn anything."

"Anyway," Trixie said, "Mart can't rely on Gordon for help, and we can't rely on Norma. We'll have to come up with something by ourselves."

"Well, okay," Jim said, straightening up in a businesslike way. "Let's start by figuring out who our natural allies are in a plan to save the birds. Have any ideas?"

"Anyone who loves animals," Di suggested.

"We need to be a little more specific," Jim said. "Anyone who loves birds . . . anyone who loves game birds. How about hunters' associations?"

"You mean ask hunters to save the birds this winter, so they can kill them next fall?" Trixie asked indignantly.

"Don't be so narrow-minded, Trix," Brian said. "Responsible hunters don't do any harm to the bird population. And they'd be willing to help save many more birds than they could ever shoot."

"Well, okay," Trixie said. "How do we reach the hunters?"

"Through their hunting dogs," Dan said.

"Jim's springer spaniel, Patch, is a hunting dog. So is the Beldens' setter, Reddy. I know the people who train those dogs are well organized. They'd be listed in the phone book."

"An excellent idea, in general," Mart said. "I feel compelled to make one minor correction, however. Reddy may have the genetic heritage of a hunting dog, but his total lack of training makes him useless for hunting as well as everything else."

There was a round of laughter from the Bob-Whites. Everyone had to agree with Mart's assessment. The Irish setter was lovable and energetic, but the energy was generally used to get into mischief rather than for any more practical purpose.

"We could also post a notice at Dr. Chang's office," Dan said. "He's an excellent veterinarian. Every animal lover in town winds up going to see him sooner or later."

"Dr. Chang might even let us tuck in a letter with the bills he sends out," Di said.

"Those are good ideas," Trixie said. "But we still need more."

"I agree," Honey said. "We need an event. If it's exciting enough, it will really get people involved in saving the birds."

"That's exactly what I was trying to say," Trixie told Honey. Turning to the other Bob-Whites, she said, "We need something that will appeal to animal lovers everywhere. But what?"

Before anyone could answer, Patch nudged open the door of the den and padded across the room to his owner. Unlike Reddy, Patch was well trained. At a word from Jim, the dog sat down quietly, panting softly as Jim scratched him behind the ear.

"Patch must be responding to your appeal to animal lovers everywhere," Jim said. "There's certainly nobody who loves game birds more than he does. You'd help if you could, wouldn't you, Patch?"

"He can!" Trixie shouted.

Startled, everyone—Patch included—turned to look at Trixie. She had set down her mug of cider and jumped to her feet. The look that everyone knew so well—the look that said Trixie Belden had just been struck by a perfect idea—had set her face aglow.

"That's exactly it," Trixie said in a slightly softer voice. "Patch *can* help us save the game birds. And so, believe it or not, can Reddy!"

# 3 * The Bob-Whites Begin

TRIXIE'S WORDS seemed to fall into a well of silence. Her friends' faces reflected a combination of surprise, anticipation, and total bewilderment. Trixie let the silence stretch on, enjoying the mystery she had created.

Even Honey, who usually could read Trixie's mind, was puzzled. "*How* can Patch and Reddy help us save the game birds?"

Trixie decided she'd kept her friends in suspense long enough. "Why, by entering the pet show we're going to have to raise money and get support for the game birds," she said.

"Think about it. The people who pay to enter the pet show, and the people who pay to attend, are bound to be animal lovers. So not only will they enjoy contributing to a good cause, they'll also be the right people to educate about feeding the birds."

Almost immediately, Honey exclaimed, "Oh, Trixie, what a wonderful idea! It's absolutely, positively brilliant!"

"Can we actually do it?" Jim asked cautiously. "It's a big project."

"Not any bigger than the antique show or the ice carnival we held a while ago, and those events were both successful," Honey pointed out.

"It does seem to me that the basic elements would be the same," Mart said. "We'd need to set a date, find a place to hold the show, and get posters and fliers printed and circulated. And, of course, we'd need to enroll pets. But that wouldn't be hard."

"See?" Trixie said. "Mart agrees with me. That means it has to be a perfect plan!"

"You weren't thinking of a formal, accredited pet show, were you? Because we don't have the expertise to do something like that," Brian said.

"Heavens, no!" Trixie said. "This one will be purely for fun, with prizes for biggest pet and smallest pet and friendliest and most unusual. Definitely *not* formal and accredited."

"That's just as well, since the Belden clan doesn't own a formal and accredited pet, anyway," Mart said dryly.

"Are you going to enter Reddy as 'most energetic'?" Honey teased.

The other Bob-Whites laughed, but Jim remained serious. "If the Bob-Whites are sponsoring the show, we'd better stay out of the entries. It wouldn't look right if we entered, let alone if we happened to win something."

"That's fine with me," Trixie agreed. "Reddy at home is pretty awful, but Reddy in public is unbearable."

"Okay," Jim said, "let's start planning." He walked over to the desk and got a yellow legal pad and a pencil. "First, the place."

"How about the school gym?" Trixie suggested.

Jim nodded and made note of the suggestion. "I'll ask the principal tomorrow. I'm pretty sure he'll say yes."

"How soon can we have the pet show?" Dan Mangan asked. "The critical time to help the birds is right now."

Jim checked the desk calendar. "It has to be on a Saturday," he said. "And we'll need a couple of Saturdays before the show to get people signed up. So I'd say two weeks from this Saturday, at the earliest."

"That long?" Trixie asked in dismay. "Thousands of birds will have died by then."

"You're forgetting one of the major strengths of this plan," Honey said reassuringly. "The idea isn't just to raise funds, it's also to raise awareness. And we'll be doing that the moment the first poster goes up. The whole time we're getting people signed up for the show, we'll also be encouraging them to feed the birds."

Trixie's gloomy look brightened a little bit. "You're right. But I can see that publicity is ten times more important for this event than for the others we've had. We'll need really good posters—and lots of them."

"Fortunately, we know an excellent artist," Brian told her.

"Nick Roberts, of course!" Trixie said. "I'll talk to him tomorrow."

"Actually, Nick Roberts's name had occurred to me in another context," Mart said.

"You mentioned all the prizes you'd like to award. It seems to me that ribbons and trophies might be just what we're looking for."

"And Roberts's Trophy Shop is one place in town where our credit is exceedingly good," Brian concluded approvingly.

"This just keeps getting better and better," Trixie said. "Let's not forget the idea of putting a flier in the bills Dr. Chang sends out. Only instead of just a request that everyone feed the birds, it can also be an invitation to the show! Hey, how about asking Dr. Chang to be the judge?"

"Good idea," Jim said. He quickly jotted it down.

"I can't wait to get started," Honey said.

"That's just as well, because we already *have* started," Jim said, turning the pad to show her a full page of notes. "And with the show just two weeks from Saturday, we're going to have to move fast."

Before the meeting ended, they had drawn up a list of tasks that included talking to the school principal, contacting Nick Roberts and Dr. Chang, and getting permission to set up a sign-up table at Sleepyside Mall the following two Saturdays.

When the meeting was over, Mart, Brian, Dan, and Di headed for home. Trixie remained behind to work with Honey on the wording of the fliers and posters.

"We need a slogan," Trixie said. "Something like, 'Help our feathered friends.' " She wrinkled her nose at her own effort. "Something like that—only not so boring and silly."

"It needs to say both things—about helping the game birds *and* coming to the pet show," Honey said. "The best description was when you said that Patch and Reddy could help save the game birds. It certainly caught our attention, and once you explained it, it made perfect sense. Only how do we say that to people who don't know Patch and Reddy?"

Trixie stared intently at her friend for a moment. Then she tore off the top sheet of the pad and began working on a fresh sheet. When she was finished, she turned the pad around to show it to Honey.

Honey immediately began to laugh.

What Trixie had drawn was a stick-figure dog, with a tail, floppy ears, and a bone in its mouth. The dog was holding the bone out to a small, two-legged animal with a curly topknot—presumably a quail. Above the draw-

ing, Trixie had lettered: HELP YOUR PET HELP
THE STARVING GAME BIRDS!

"I'll be ashamed to show this to Nick, because he's such a good artist," Trixie said.

"Don't be. If he's been in any danger of taking his talent for granted, this will remind him
of how special he is." Honey made her obser-
vation in her usual tactful way. Only the merri-
ment in her eyes showed that she was teasing
her friend.

The Bob-Whites found Nick Roberts in the
school art studio the next morning before
class.

"Very good," Nick said when Trixie handed
him her sketch. "I think I'll be able to do
something nice with it. The pet show is a good
idea, too. I saw an article in the paper about
the trouble the game birds are in, and I've
wanted to help without knowing how. Could
we donate some ribbons and trophies as
prizes for the show?"

"Oh!" Trixie widened her blue eyes in
mock surprise. "Gee—I hadn't thought of it,
but that's a good idea, too. Isn't it, gang?"

As the others mumbled their agreement,
Jim took a long list and a pencil out of his shirt

pocket. Elaborately, he made a big check mark next to one item. " 'Ask Nick for ribbons and trophies'—done," he said.

Nick began to laugh. "One step ahead of me, as usual. Since you folks are usually headed in the right direction, I don't mind."

"Thank you, Nick," Honey said, acknowledging both Nick's help and his compliment. "I hope all the other things on Jim's list will be as easy to accomplish."

After school, the young people piled into the Bob-White station wagon, a gift to the club from Matthew Wheeler. After a whole day outside, the car was so cold that the engine turned over slowly.

"I know just how it feels," Trixie grumbled.

"Oh, no, you don't," Jim retorted. "This slow-starting car has nothing in common with the Bob-Whites. Why, we're less than twenty-four hours into our planning for the pet show, and just look what we've accomplished. I saw the principal and he gave us permission to use the gym and have a sign-up table in the main hall. Nick is doing posters and contributing ribbons. We're off and rolling. Next stop—Dr. Chang's."

Dr. Chang's office was a squat, brick building that sat by itself on the outskirts of town. The isolation was necessary because, for most of the day, dogs barked at one another in the waiting room. Their barking created more barking from the dogs who were recovering from illness or being boarded in the kennel at the back of the building.

"It's deafening," Trixie said as the Bob-Whites approached the door. "I don't know how he stands it."

"He probably doesn't even hear it anymore," Di said. "You can get used to lots of noise, believe me." Di, who had a set of younger twin brothers *and* a set of younger twin sisters, made a wry face.

Inside, the temperature was cool, set for the comfort of furry animals, not humans. In the waiting room, the pets' owners sat with their coats on. A well-trained Doberman pinscher sat quietly, watching everything without moving. An energetic terrier ran in short circles permitted by its leash. A tiny Chihuahua sat in its owner's lap, trembling despite its knit sweater. A gray cat, wrapped in a green towel, rested in its owner's arms.

All of the animals and their owners turned to stare at the Bob-Whites, and Trixie felt self-conscious as she walked over to the reception window. "We're here to see Dr. Chang," she said. "We called him this morning, and he said to come over after school."

"I'll tell him you're here," the receptionist said.

The pets and their owners continued to stare at the seven young people, none of whom had a pet. When the receptionist finally escorted them into Dr. Chang's office, Trixie felt both relieved to get away and guilty for taking up someone else's appointment time.

"This won't take long," she assured him as she and her friends crowded into the office. She explained the pet show idea to Dr. Chang and soon had him nodding his enthusiasm.

Honey explained the idea of enclosing fliers with his monthly statements, and the veterinarian nodded again. "You caught me just in time. Statements go out on the tenth, which is Friday. If you give me the fliers before that, I'll be happy to include them."

"Now there's just one more thing," Trixie said. "We want you to judge the pet show."

Dr. Chang looked at Trixie through his thick, wire-rimmed glasses. "I already have half of Sleepyside angry with me because I tell them that their animals are overweight or not well groomed. Or I anger them by saying they should keep their dogs on leashes so I don't have to stitch up cuts and gashes. If those judgments upset them, what will my judgments at the pet show do?"

"Oh, but this isn't that kind of pet show," Honey said. "Roberts's Trophy Shop is supplying us with lots of ribbons and trophies. Every animal that enters will get something, so their owners will all go home happy."

"All?" Dr. Chang asked.

"All," Mart said quickly. "We'll have enough trophies for every animal. As the entries come in, we'll figure out a winning category for each."

"All right," Dr. Chang said. "I may live to regret this, but I'll do it."

"Yippee!" Trixie shouted, and her friends chorused their thank-you's.

"We're off to Sleepyside Mall now," Jim said to Dr. Chang. "We'll bring you the fliers by Friday."

Outside, Trixie sighed with relief. "Whew! For a minute there, I thought we'd hit our first real snag. I'm glad we managed to talk him into it."

"I'm afraid we may have said too much," Brian said as he slid into the front seat of the station wagon next to Jim.

"What do you mean?" Honey asked.

"I mean that my outspoken younger brother promised Dr. Chang that we'd devise a separate category for each animal. That's a lot of categories. Imagine sorting through all the entries to find the largest pet, then going through them again to find the smallest, and on and on, over and over again."

"Such lengthy labors will be unnecessary," Mart said. "You see, yesterday in my computer programming class the teacher announced that we each have to come up with our own program. I've been wondering what mine would be. As soon as Honey mentioned all the prizes at the pet show, I realized that computerization was in order—indeed, indispensable. All we need to do is have each entrant fill out a detailed entry blank, with height, weight, type of animal, and special characteristics. I input the data into a program I've devised that will subsort by predefined categories. Then, the morning of the contest, I push a button, and it all prints out in a matter of seconds."

"Really?" Trixie asked, genuinely impressed. "The computer can do all that?"

"The *program* can, if I write it that way," Mart corrected her.

"It's hard to imagine," Honey said.

"Well, when the time comes, I'll let you watch while I run the program," Mart promised.

When they arrived at the mall, everyone piled out of the car. Mart ran all the way to the main entrance, so he could get in out of the cold.

"What did people do before there were indoor shopping malls?" Trixie wondered aloud, as she ran into the mall behind her brother.

"They probably did a lot less shopping," Brian replied.

The mall was laid out like the letter I. The top and bottom of the I, each four stories high, were Sleepyside's two big department stores. The two-story center area that connected them was lined with smaller stores, each with its own specialty: cheeses, candles, jewelry, fabrics, sports equipment.

The Bob-Whites quickly fanned out to accomplish as much as possible in a short time.

Within a half hour, they were gathered around a table in the snack bar, soft drinks in hand, toasting the success of their efforts.

"We can have the sign-up table right outside the pet store," Jim said.

"The owner promised to have plenty of cracked corn on hand," Mart added, "as well as instructions on the care and feeding of game birds, so people will know just what to do."

"*And* we have spots reserved for twenty posters," Trixie reported. "I think the pet show is going to be the Bob-Whites' most successful event yet."

Over the next couple of days, the truth of Trixie's prediction became clear. On Thursday afternoon, Nick Roberts presented Trixie with a stack of posters that delighted her. The stick-figure dog she'd drawn had turned into a beautiful, intelligent-looking retriever. Nick had even managed to put a wag into the dog's tail. And the tiny quail was so adorable and fragile-looking that it seemed to say, "Feed me."

"Oh, Nick, thank you!" Trixie said.

"Thank *you*," Nick replied. "It's nice to feel

that I'm helping you and your friends for a change, instead of the other way around."

Trixie took the posters directly to the school office. It was a strict policy at Sleepyside Junior-Senior High School that all posters had to be initialed by Miss von Trammel, the school secretary. The procedure itself was easy. Miss von Trammel always smiled, admired the artistry of the posters—whether it was admirable or not—and quickly initialed each one.

At least, that's what Trixie had always known her to do in the past. And that's what she seemed about to do this time. Then, suddenly, she froze, holding her pen motionless a couple of inches above the top poster.

"Dr. Chang." Miss von Trammel almost spit out the words.

"Yes," Trixie said. "He's our judge!"

"That—that quack!" Miss von Trammel said angrily. "He's no judge of animals. He shouldn't even be allowed near them!"

"W-what?" Trixie stammered, bewildered. "But he's—he's a veterinarian."

"He's a quack," Miss von Trammel repeated.

Still the pen remained unmoving above the stack of posters. For a moment, Trixie wondered if the secretary would refuse to initial them.

At last, Miss von Trammel brought the pen down on the first poster—with almost a stabbing motion—and signed it, then the next, then the next.

Trixie stood watching, wondering what she should say. When the initialing was completed, she settled for a quick thank-you. Then she grabbed the posters and hurried out of the school office.

"It was totally unlike her," Trixie told Honey after school as the two of them made the rounds of the hallways, putting up the posters. "What could there be about Dr. Chang to make her react so violently?"

"Maybe she doesn't like him because he's Oriental," Honey speculated as she tore off a strip of masking tape, turned it into a loop, and mounted it on the back of a poster.

"Ugh—you don't really think that's it, do you?" Trixie said as she put the poster up against the wall and smoothed it down.

"No, come to think of it, I don't. We have people of many different races here at school. I've never seen Miss von Trammel seem rude or unfriendly to any of them."

"It's pretty mysterious," Trixie said as she picked up the stack of posters and headed on down the hall.

"Ah-ah-ah!" Honey warned. "No mysteries this time, remember?"

"You're right again," Trixie agreed. "Much as I love a mystery, there's no time to investigate one now. The pet show is our number-one-and-only priority."

# 4 * The Angry Young Man

Trixie found it easy to keep her pledge, for the pet show took up all of her time. On Friday, the Bob-Whites had their first sign-up at school. Honey, Trixie, and Di agreed to handle that chore. The table was mobbed with eager students for two solid hours, making the girls wish the boys were there, too.

"I had no idea so many people were pet lovers," Honey said.

"*I* had no idea so many people were dying of boredom this winter," Trixie replied. "I think that has as much to do with it as anything. If we'd let them sign up to watch paint dry in the auditorium one whole Saturday afternoon, I think we'd have gotten nearly as many entrants."

"I don't know if I'd go *that* far," said one of the boys who was filling out an entry blank. "But if it was a sunny Saturday in June, I probably wouldn't be entering my brother's hamster in a pet show, either!" Grinning, he thrust his entry blank and two dollars at Trixie.

"Houdini?" Trixie read in surprise.

"My brother named him that the third time he wriggled out of his cage. He's a great escape artist, get it?" the boy said.

"I get it, but I wish I hadn't. You'll make sure Houdini doesn't escape the day of the show, won't you?" Trixie pleaded.

"Sure, although if we spent the next couple of months chasing a hamster through the halls, it would make the winter go that much quicker." Seeing Trixie's face turn pale, he held up a soothing hand. "Just kidding," he said. "See you at the show."

"Houdini the hamster," Trixie muttered as he walked away. "At least that name makes sense, once it's explained. But some of these others! Max the wonder dog. Veronica the cat." Trixie shook her head in disbelief.

"Nothing sensible, like Reddy or Patch, you mean?" Di teased.

"Those names make perfect sense," Trixie said. "Reddy is an Irish setter, so he's red. Patch has brown and white patches. What else would you call them?"

Di shrugged. "It's the *kinds* of pets that I find hard to believe. I'd expected lots of cats and dogs, but we already have entries for parakeets, canaries, hamsters, guinea pigs, a ferret, two gerbils, and I don't know what else."

"Here's the entry for my python," a rangy teenager said, handing the slip of paper to Di.

Di reached for the entry form, then pulled her hand back fast. "A snake?" she asked, looking at the entry as if the piece of paper itself might be coiled to strike.

"Scott Hopper, I don't believe you for a moment," Trixie said, pulling the paper out of his hand. She read what he had printed on it: " 'Ed, an orange tabby cat.' " Di took the entry gingerly, then sighed with relief as she read it and realized that Trixie was telling the truth, while Scott had been teasing.

"Like you said, it's been a boring winter," Scott told the girls with a grin. "I just wanted to liven things up a little bit." He handed over his two dollars and walked away.

"That was a close call," Honey said. "But what if somebody *does* try to enter a snake?"

"We have to let them enter," Trixie said. "We didn't say 'no snakes' on the poster."

Trixie's mind was taken off snakes when she spotted someone standing in the hallway a short distance from their table. She nudged Honey and whispered, "Look over there."

"Norma Nelson," Honey said. "She must be about ready to go feed the birds—she's dressed for it, anyway."

"That's what I thought," Trixie said. "But this is the *third* time I've looked up and seen her."

"You mean she just keeps standing there?" Honey asked.

Trixie shook her head. "She leaves and comes back, I think. I've looked up a few times and she hasn't been there."

"Maybe she's the forgetful type," Di said. "Sometimes I have to go back to my locker three times before I get everything I need."

"Maybe," Trixie said reluctantly. "But there's something kind of creepy about the way she's standing there."

"Oooh, don't say 'creepy,'" Di said, hugging herself and shuddering. "You're making me think of snakes again. This pet show just isn't as much fun as it used to be."

By the next day, though, Di found it hard to maintain her pessimistic attitude. At the end of the first hour she spent at the sign-up table at Sleepyside Mall, her eyes were sparkling. "At school, it was the pets that seemed funny," she whispered to Trixie. "Here, it's the own-ers!"

Trixie nodded her agreement. She handed an entry blank to a middle-aged couple who were decked out in matching snowmobile suits. "Dr. Chang was right," she whispered back. "People do take their pets seriously. That's what seems so funny."

As if to illustrate Trixie's point, the woman looked up from the entry blank and said, "This competition won't be too strenuous, will it? Our Samantha is a very intelligent cat, but she isn't overly physical, if you know what I mean."

Struggling to keep a straight face, Trixie an-swered, "No, ma'am. The animals don't really need to *do* anything, except be there. Intelligence counts every bit as much as, uh, *physique* in this show."

"Well, then, Ward, we certainly want to enter Samantha," the woman said. Her husband nodded, and the woman filled out the entry blank and handed it back to Trixie with their two dollars.

When they had left, Trixie said, "Well, the grown-ups in Sleepyside are sillier about their pets than the teenagers are. I'd say they're just as bored with winter, though, judging from the activity we've had today."

"The pet show is bound to be a success, all right," Di agreed.

"It will be successful in every way," Honey added. "I've seen several people go inside the pet shop after we've talked to them and come out with sacks of cracked corn. So we're helping the game birds already!"

"So you're helping the game birds." The mocking voice made the three girls look up with a start. A thin, bearded young man was standing in front of their table. Unlike most of the people at the mall, he was wearing a thin, woolen jacket, not a thick, down-filled one. He was bare-headed, and there were no bulges in his pockets from heavy gloves. "The birds will be fed this winter. Isn't that just wonderful."

"We think it is," Trixie said.

"Sure, it is," the young man said in the same sarcastic way. "Let's be sure we save the birds, the adorable little birds. Let's not worry about all the *people* in the world who are starving. They aren't *cute*. They don't *sing* pretty for the folks here in Sleepyside. So it's no point seeing that they get fed."

"That's not true," Trixie said, her temper flaring. "We *have* raised money for people. We *do* think people are important. We just happen to be helping the birds this time, that's all."

"You've done your bit for people, have you? Is that what you're trying to say?" the young man retorted.

"That's not it at all," Honey said. "We haven't done enough for people. I mean, not all we're ever going to do. We'll do more someday, but— Oh, what's the use of talking to you?"

"None at all," said another voice.

The girls turned to see a middle-aged man approaching the table. He was as distinguished-looking as the younger man was scruffy. His charcoal-gray topcoat made his curly white hair seem almost radiant. He held his hat politely in his hands. "He won't listen to you, no matter how long or how hard you try to talk to him. His sort are interested in finding problems, not in solving them," the older man said.

"You call this a solution?" the young man said. With a wave of his arm, he dismissed the girls, the sign-up table, the entry blanks, and the posters.

"I call it a good start," the older man said calmly. "If you don't like it, why don't you go off somewhere and see if you can come up with something better?"

The young man opened his mouth to make another sarcastic retort. Something in his confronter's calm but determined gaze seemed to stop him. Without another word, he turned and strode angrily away from the table.

"Whew! I guess that's what they call an angry young man!" Trixie said.

"You handled him beautifully," Honey said. "We would have sat here all day, trying to defend ourselves."

"Don't ever feel you need to defend yourself from blowhards like that," the older man said. His voice was soft and calm, but the gleam in his eyes showed the intensity of his feelings. "If he really cared about others, he'd find a way to help—as you girls have. Instead, he *pretends* to care about others as a way of calling attention to himself."

"I'd never thought of it that way, but I think you're right," Trixie said.

"I *know* I am. Now, may I make a donation to your cause, just in case the young rebel frightened away some potential donors?" He reached into his breast pocket and pulled out a large leather wallet.

"Well, you don't really *donate*," Trixie explained. "You pay a fee for entering your pet in the pet show, and that's how we raise money."

The man put his head back and laughed loudly. "My pets are two very aged and placid cocker spaniels. Their show days are long past. I'm sure that they would prefer it if I just gave you some money and let them stay home."

"I can understand that," Trixie said, grinning at him. "My dog will be staying home the day of the contest, too, but not because he's placid. In fact, he's so energetic he'd probably destroy the gym."

The man had taken a bill out of his wallet.

As Trixie spoke, he took out another one. "In that case," he said, "let me make a contribution in your dog's name, as well." He handed over the money, nodded to the girls, and walked away.

"There's forty dollars here!" Trixie gasped. "Two twenty-dollar bills. See?"

"That's as much money as *twenty* entries in the show!" Honey exclaimed.

"What a wonderful man!" Di said.

Trixie nodded, then she said thoughtfully, "We actually owe this forty dollars to that loud-mouthed man who attracted the *nice* man to our table." She broke into a grin. "If you don't mind, though, I'm not going to go track him down to thank him."

The girls' laughter was interrupted by the arrival of more entrants in the show, and the next few hours passed quickly as the table stayed busy. By the time Brian came to get the girls in his car, they'd signed up forty-two entries.

"Added to the thirty we signed up at school, that's seventy-two pets. And we still have two more weeks to get entries!" Trixie said enthusiastically.

She repeated her good news to her brothers that evening as they all sat in the den watching the news on television. "At this rate, we won't need any help from you boys at all," Trixie said.

"I congratulate you on your success at the sign-up booth," Mart said. "But might I remind you that I spent that same period of time in the computer room at school, working on the program for the pet show?"

"Is it almost ready?" Trixie asked.

"Almost," Mart said. "There are still a few glitches to be straightened out, but the teacher says that's to be expected in undertaking a task of this complexity."

"Good," Trixie said. "Because we'll have a lot of pets and a lot of categories. I had no idea people owned so many different " She paused as the picture on the television screen caught her eye. "It's him!" she shouted.

"It's who?" Brian asked.

"I don't know. I mean, I don't know his name. Turn up the sound and let's find out."

Brian turned the knob, and Trixie heard a familiar voice: "People are starving to death all over the world today. *Today*, when technology has grown to such proportions that no task as basic as feeding humanity should be beyond our grasp."

The face of the man disappeared from the screen, and the television news reporter came on. "Those were the words today of Paul Gale, the noted anti-hunger crusader," she said. "Gale, whose World Anti-Hunger Foundation raises money to buy supplies that are flown directly to Burma, Thailand, and other Third-World countries, will be in Sleepyside for the next several weeks to assist in the opening of a foundation office here. Gale said he chose our community because its relative prosperity should permit large donations to those less fortunate."

The reporter's face was replaced by Paul Gale's. He looked serious—and very angry. "People who have the most must share the most. Why, here in Sleepyside people have so much that they're literally throwing their money to the birds. This, while children are dying. Something must be done!"

The camera stayed on Paul Gale's face while the reporter said, "Those interested in making contributions may mail them to the World

Anti-Hunger Foundation, Seventy-five South Tenth Street."

The news program moved on to other events, but Trixie didn't hear them. "That was our pet show he was talking about when he said people are throwing money to the birds!" Briefly, she told her brothers about her encounter with Paul Gale at the sign-up table. "He's going to wreck the whole pet show if he keeps talking like that," she concluded worriedly.

"I doubt it," Brian told her. "His worthy cause doesn't make ours any less worthy. People will understand that."

"Maybe you're right," Trixie conceded. "It's just that things have been going so well. I'd hate to see us run into problems now."

# 5 * Honey Uncovers a Rumor

THE FOLLOWING WEEK, Trixie realized that the pet show *was* having serious problems.

At school Monday, the flow of entrants at the sign-up table slowed to a trickle. "That's okay," Trixie said as she and Brian packed away the meager stack of dollar bills they'd taken in. "We have enough pets now. Even if no one else signs up this week, the show will be a success."

But on Tuesday, things got worse — entrants began withdrawing from the contest. The first withdrawal was by a girl with a pet parakeet.

"They're very prone to respiratory infections," she said. "They're tropical birds, originally, you know. So my mom says it wouldn't be a good idea to take Peewee out in the cold."

The excuse sounded logical, and Trixie obligingly found Peewee's entry blank, tore it in two, and gave the girl her money back.

Almost immediately, another student came up to the table. "I'll be visiting my grandmother that day," he said. "So I can't bring my cat. Could I withdraw from the show?"

Trixie realized that she'd set a dangerous precedent with Peewee; there was no choice but to return the money.

Three more students withdrew by the end of the day, all with increasingly lame-sounding excuses.

"I don't understand it," Trixie said to Honey. "Do you think that TV interview with Paul Gale is what started this?"

Honey, looking disappointed, tried to be cheerful. "I doubt it. Someone would have mentioned his name. I think there was such a rush of enthusiasm, people didn't stop to think before they entered. Now that they've had a chance to think it over and tell their parents about it, there are bound to be a few snags."

There were indeed four more "snags" the following day, reducing the total number of entrants to less than seventy.

By now, even Honey was finding it difficult to stay calm about the withdrawals. "This isn't a normal drop-out rate," she said. "Something's going on, and I'm going to find out what it is."

"How are you going to do that?" Trixie asked.

Honey's jaw set in a stubborn look that was rare for her. "I'll think of a way," she replied.

A few moments later a girl from Honey's homeroom withdrew her dog. This girl, too, had suddenly found out about a visit to her grandparents on the day of the show.

Honey managed to smile as she returned the money. Calmly, she watched the girl walk away from the sign-up table. Then she stood up and said, "You wait here, Trixie. I'm going to talk to Heather."

Honey followed the girl. Trixie saw Heather turn and pause as Honey quietly called her name. The two girls talked for several minutes.

Finally, Heather went off down the hall. Honey walked back toward the sign-up table. A tight knot formed in Trixie's stomach as

Honey drew nearer. There was a smile on Honey's face—but there were tears in her eyes!

"Oh, Trixie," she said softly, the tears running down her cheeks, "you won't believe this. She says there's a rumor going around school about us, and that's why she withdrew. The rumor is that we don't plan to use this money for the game birds at all—we're going to spend it on ourselves!"

Trixie was absolutely stunned. "We're going to have to tell the other Bob-Whites right away," she said. "This is too big—and too awful—for us to handle on our own." She began to sweep the contents of the sign-up table into piles that she and Honey could carry to their lockers for storage.

Just as the girls were finishing, Jim appeared in the hallway. "What's up, sis? I came back early to help you with the sign-up, but the table's gone. This is no time for you and Trixie to take a vacation," he added with a teasing grin.

As Honey turned to face him, Jim's grin faded. Seeing her distraught, tear-streaked face, he asked, "Honey, what is it? What's happened?"

Honey swallowed hard and shook her head.

"I can't tell you. I mean, I *have* to tell you, but I need to tell the other Bob-Whites, too, and I can't say it more than once. We need an emergency meeting right away."

"Right away," Trixie echoed lamely.

Without further question, Jim said, "Let's head home. But first, I'll call Brian and Mart to tell them we'll be stopping by for them. I'll have them call Di and see if she can get a ride to the Manor House. We can just swing by Mr. Maypenny's on our way; Dan will probably be there. Head for the station wagon—it's unlocked. I'll catch up."

Trixie's feet were leaden as she moved toward the door. *At least he didn't make us explain*, she thought. *And at least he's still able to think clearly, even though Honey and I can't.*

The girls were barely seated in the car before Jim opened the door on the driver's side and took his place behind the wheel. "Brian and Mart will pick up Di and meet us at home," he said. "That will give us time to get Dan."

The drive out of Sleepyside and along Glen Road seemed endless. Trixie alternated between trying frantically to think of a way to end the rumors about the pet show, and trying just as frantically to put the whole thing out of her mind until the Bob-Whites were all assembled.

The only distraction was Honey's nudging her and pointing to the side of the road. There, a hen and a rooster pheasant were picking along a thin strip of ground.

"Poor things," Honey said softly. "All we wanted to do was help."

*From the way she put it,* Trixie thought, *I can't tell if she means the pheasants are the "poor things" or we are. Maybe she means it both ways. I think we're more like sitting ducks than pheasants, though—for whoever started this stupid rumor.*

Soon they pulled up in front of the cabin where Dan lived with Mr. Maypenny, and Jim ran in to get Dan. The two boys were back in minutes, and Dan had been told not to ask any questions.

It took only moments to drive from Mr. Maypenny's to the Manor House. Trixie noted with relief that Brian's car was parked out front.

Brian, Mart, and Di were already waiting in the den. Trixie and Honey took off their coats and sat down close together on the couch. Honey looked at her more-talkative friend, but Trixie shook her head. "You're the one who heard it firsthand. You tell them."

"A girl named Heather told me about a rumor that's spreading through school," Honey said. "The rumor is that we're going to use the pet show money for ourselves, not for the game birds."

Trixie waited for a burst of protest, but there was none. Apparently, her friends were as bewildered by the explanation as she had been earlier.

"Maybe we can track the rumor to its source and stamp it out," Dan said finally. "Did your friend say where she heard it?"

Honey shook her head. "I asked her that, but she can't remember where she heard it the first time."

"The first time?" Brian echoed, recognizing immediately the significance of those words.

"That's right," Honey said, confirming his fears. "Apparently, the rumor is absolutely all over school. Everybody has heard it from three or four different people by now. There's no way of knowing how it started, so there's no way of stopping it."

"The former is true," Mart said. "The latter is not. There must be a way of stopping the rumor, and we'll figure out what it is."

"The solution is to prove to people that the pet show is strictly on the up-and-up," Dan said.

"Right," Brian said, nodding approvingly. "But how?"

"I think I've got something," Trixie said.

"Say on," Mart told her.

"Well, if people don't trust us with the pet show money, we shouldn't *have* the pet show money," Trixie said. "Why couldn't we set up an account at the bank? I'm sure we could arrange things so that we can't take any money out without the bank's knowledge and permission. Then people don't have to trust us—they can just trust the bank."

"Oh, Trixie, that's perfectly perfect!" Honey said enthusiastically.

"Yes, that should do it," Brian said. "And to announce the plan, we'll just need to print up more fliers."

"All those in favor of Trixie's plan, signify by saying aye," Jim said.

"Aye!" everyone chorused.

"Motion carried," Jim said.

"I move that we adjourn, so that the Belden Bob-Whites can talk to their father about setting up an account for the pet show proceeds," Dan said. "Mr. Belden is an officer of the bank, after all."

"I'll second that motion," Honey said.

"I'll call you later," Trixie said, jumping up from the couch and pulling on her coat as she dashed for the door.

Her two older brothers, normally less impulsive, were right behind her.

# 6 * Dr. Chang Explains

"IT'S WORKING!" Honey exclaimed the next afternoon, as the tenth student in less than half an hour walked away from the sign-up table.

"It's better than working," Trixie replied. "I think the sign-up is going better now than it was before the rumor started."

"You're right," Honey agreed. "Every student in school must have seen the fliers we circulated this morning, describing our new arrangement with the bank. That must have reassured the students who were believing the rumor. And the fliers also reminded the students who'd been meaning to sign up and hadn't gotten around to it."

"Just don't expect me to be grateful for the rumor," Trixie said. "I keep remembering how awful it was. Who would hate the Bob-Whites that much?"

"Maybe no one," said Honey. "Jim and I talked about it last night after you and your brothers left. You know, sometimes somebody makes a joke or wonders aloud about something. Another person overhears and takes it as truth, and that person repeats it. Pretty soon it's a full-fledged rumor. But it's not vicious, and it's not intentional."

Trixie shook her head. "I'm sure that happens sometimes. But not this time. Someone started that rumor deliberately to hurt the Bob-Whites." There was a mystery here— Trixie just knew it!

"All right," said Honey. "Maybe it's the pet show that's the target, not the Bob-Whites at all."

"That's possible," Trixie said.

"But who hates the pet show?" Honey asked.

Trixie was one step ahead of her friend. "I can think of two suspects. Paul Gale has publicly attacked the pet show twice—at the mall

and on TV. And Miss von Trammel was furious
about Dr. Chang being the judge."

"I'll admit that Paul Gale seems to hate the
pet show—or rather, the bird-feeding plan.
He couldn't have started the rumor, though,
because he doesn't have access to the school,
where the rumor started. As for Miss von
Trammel, I can't believe she'd be so angry that
she'd want to ruin the whole show."

"I saw her, you didn't," Trixie countered.
"She was plenty angry."

"I've seen her nearly every school day since
I moved to Sleepyside, though," said Honey.
"I just can't believe she'd suddenly become
such a—such a raving maniac."

"A distinct description of my distaff sib-
ling," Mart said, as he and Brian came to re-
lieve the girls at the sign-up table.

"Not Trixie," Honey said, "Miss—"

"Missed you here at the table," Trixie said
quickly. "Glad you've finally come. Really
busy here. Good luck." As she spoke, she
picked her books up from the floor, then
tucked them under her arm. "Come on,
Honey. Let's let the men do some work for a
change."

A new flock of students coming up to the table distracted the boys. Honey waited until

they were out of earshot to ask, "What's up?"

"You said you can't imagine Miss von Trammel that angry. I'm going to show you how angry she can get," Trixie said. From the bottom of her pile of books, she produced a thin stack of fliers that she'd secretly picked up from the sign-up table. Waving them in the air like a battle flag, she said, "Follow me."

The two girls trooped into the school office. They stood in front of the counter, waiting for Miss von Trammel to look up from her desk. When the secretary saw them, she bustled over to them immediately.

"I'm sorry to bother you so late in the day," Trixie said, "but we need to have these fliers initialed, so we can put them up on the bulletin board."

Miss von Trammel took one of the fliers and read it.

Trixie watched her closely. *I have to try to make Miss von Trammel really angry again,* Trixie thought, *so Honey can see—even though it's a mean thing to do.* Trixie cleared her throat before she spoke aloud. "We had these printed up because there was a rumor that the pet show wasn't on the up-and-up. Can you imagine—when we have the town's best veterinarian doing the judging?" Trixie hoped she sounded more innocent than she felt.

Miss von Trammel's face hardened into a gray mask. *I always thought that was just an expression—but she really does look as though she'd been carved out of stone*, Trixie thought. Her stomach tightened with guilt as she realized that she'd brought that change about deliberately.

"Dr. Chang is a quack. I told you that before," Miss von Trammel said sharply. "Any negative rumor about him would be very easy to believe. As for these fliers, I'd say everyone in school must have seen them by now. There were certainly enough of them littering the halls. Since you didn't bother to get my permission before you handed them out, I'm going to withhold my permission for you to post them. Someone has to teach you young people that rules are meant to be obeyed." She tried to speak calmly, but two bright red spots had appeared high on her cheeks. Without another word, she turned and walked back to her desk.

Trixie and Honey quickly left the office. "You see?" Trixie hissed. "Didn't I tell you she was angry about the pet show?"

"You're right about her not liking Dr. Chang," Honey said. "That's a mystery I'd like cleared up. We're going over to Dr. Chang's office after school anyway. Let's ask him why Miss von Trammel has such strong feelings against him. Maybe then we'll know whether she's the one who's sabotaging the pet show."

Only Honey, Trixie, Jim, and Brian went to Dr. Chang's office that afternoon. Di and Dan, busy with chores, had taken the first bus home. Mart, still trying to fix his computer program, was staying at school and taking the second bus.

Jim parked the station wagon in the empty parking lot in front of the veterinarian's office. At the sound of the slamming car door, a dog began to bark. A second, a third, and then countless other dogs chimed in. As the Bob-Whites opened the door of the office, they were struck by what seemed to be a solid wall of noise.

Dr. Chang greeted the young people in the reception area. "I left the door unlocked for you, even though it's past office hours. Somehow," he said with a smile, "I didn't think you'd be able to take me by surprise. Come on back to the office."

As they followed him, the noise gradually dropped off. Finally it was quiet again.

Crowded into Dr. Chang's tiny office, the Bob-Whites quickly reviewed the plans for the pet show and the progress to date.

"The worst problem we've encountered so far," Honey said casually, "is that we've irritated the school secretary by distributing fliers without getting her permission first. Miss von Trammel was very upset about it."

"Miss von Trammel—that's the secretary's name. Do you know her, by any chance?" Trixie added.

"Yes, Miss von Trammel and I know each other," Dr. Chang said. "She was one of my first clients when I came to Sleepyside. She had an Irish setter, like the Beldens' Reddy. Rather better behaved, though.

"Rusty was a beautiful animal. He was well trained and well treated. Miss von Trammel loved him." Dr. Chang's face grew sad as he spoke.

"What happened?" Trixie asked, breaking a short but heavy silence.

"Well, in the end, she killed the dog with love. You see, Rusty had a tumor. The lump appeared on the dog's side, and Miss von Trammel tried for a long time—too long—to ignore it. I suppose she thought that it would go away by itself.

"By the time she faced the truth and brought the dog to me, it was too late. I did what I could. She wanted me to do more. Finally I told her there was nothing more to be done. I told her the animal should be put down, to end its suffering."

"Is that what she did?" Trixie asked.

"Eventually," Dr. Chang said, "after she took the dog to another vet who said the same thing. By then, however, she'd decided I'd wasted time trying ineffective treatments. She said she could have saved the dog by taking it to the other vet first. It wasn't true, of course. But I suppose it eased the guilt she felt about ignoring the tumor for so long."

"So she killed her own dog and blamed it on you," Trixie said bluntly.

"I think your way of putting it is too strong," Dr. Chang told Trixie. "I don't know that I could have saved the dog if she'd brought it to me immediately. But she did blame me for the dog's death."

"That was so long ago," Honey said. "You'd think she'd be over her anger by now."

"It really wasn't anger, though," Dr. Chang said. "I think it was guilt. That feeling tends to last quite a while—forever, sometimes."

"Poor Miss von Trammel," Honey murmured.

Dr. Chang's story seemed to cast a pall of sadness over the room. The young people finished their discussion, said good-bye to Dr. Chang, and headed for the car.

As soon as they were on their way home, however, Jim said briskly, "What's the idea of bringing up Miss von Trammel? You two girls were fishing for something. What was it?"

"We still think the rumor about the pet show was started deliberately," Trixie said. "We wanted to find out if Miss von Trammel was a likely suspect."

Jim looked puzzled. "And?" he asked leadingly.

Trixie blew out a long sigh. "And it looks like we were wrong. Anybody who once loved a dog that much wouldn't try to sabotage a pet show that's raising money to keep animals from starving."

"It's good to see you backing away from a conclusion, instead of jumping to one," Jim said.

The playful comment made Trixie's temper flare. "Just because I was wrong about Miss von Trammel doesn't mean I'm wrong about the rumor. Somebody started it, and I'm going to find out who did—with your help or without it!"

## 7 * The Man from the Mall

IN THE SCHOOL CAFETERIA the next day, the Bob-Whites made it clear that they would have no part of a mystery.

"The pet show is only a week and a half away," Jim said. "We have to give it all our energy, so we can get everything done in time."

"We can't afford any wild-goose chases," Brian said. He paused and smiled at his unintentional pun. "Not if we want to save the pheasants."

"I have barely enough time to give to the

pet show," Dan said. "I can't investigate a rumor, too."

"I heartily concur," Mart said. "The mysteries of subsorts are the *only* sort I can devote my attention to."

"Does that mean you're still having computer problems?" Di asked.

"A few minor discrepancies continue to plague me. I shall set them to rest in the next day or two," Mart said.

"You'd better," Trixie said. "Otherwise, there surely won't be any wild-goose chases, because our goose will be *cooked*."

Trixie's joke was met with loud groans.

"Okay, back to the business at hand," Jim said. "I ran into Nick Roberts this morning. He wants us to drop by his father's shop and pick out the trophies and ribbons we want for the show. Who's going to go, and when?"

"The sooner the better," Brian said.

"For sure, except I'm really busy this afternoon," Mart said through an enormous mouthful of sandwich. "I'll be closeted with the computer, as usual."

"I have to take the first bus home," Dan said.

"I do, too. Sorry," Di added.

"Well, there's still four of us," Jim said.

"Two of whom need to man the sign-up table," Brian pointed out.

"Ah-ha! Then Honey and I get to go to the store and pick out the trophies," Trixie said, rising quickly from the table.

"How did you reach that conclusion?" Jim asked.

"Well, if someone's going to *man* the table, it has to be you and Brian, doesn't it? Meanwhile, the women will be downtown picking out ribbons. We'll be back here in time for our ride home. See you!" Before the boys could protest, Trixie gathered up her lunch refuse and headed for her locker.

"Brr!" Honey said as she and Trixie started off on foot for downtown Sleepyside. "Maybe we should have let the boys do this, since they could have taken the car."

"Huh-uh. We've done more than our share of sitting at that sign-up table. We started this whole project because we were sick of being stuck indoors, so why get stuck at school?"

"It is good exercise," said Honey, pulling her head down into the protective collar of her jacket. "The store isn't far, anyway."

"N-o-o. And if we get too cold, we can al-

ways stop in someplace to warm up," Trixie
said in an overly casual tone.

Unable to turn her head in her bulky coat,
Honey looked at Trixie out of the corner of her
eye. "Just what kind of someplace did you
have in mind?" she asked.

"Oh, I don't know. Someplace where people wouldn't mind giving shelter. Someplace
where the people are, you know, charitable.
Someplace like, um, the World Anti-Hunger
Foundation."

"So that's it!" Honey said. "I wondered why
you were so eager to run this errand. But,
Trixie, you know what the boys said, and
they're right. We don't have time—"

"To chase wild geese," Trixie said. "I know,
I know. But we won't be any good to the pet
show if we get frostbite. The foundation office
is right on the way; I checked the phone book.
We'll stop on the way back from Roberts's
Trophy Shop. C'mon—let's hurry." Trixie
picked up her pace, and she kept the pace
brisk enough so that Honey couldn't protest.

By the time they reached the trophy shop,
Trixie felt warm under her layers of woolen
clothes.

The shop was cozy and comfortable. Unlike

the previous store, which had burned down, this one was bright and cheerful, even on a bleak winter day. There was more display space, and the colorful T-shirts and hats that had helped to make the store successful were pinned up on the walls.

Nick came out of the back room and smiled when he saw the girls. "Surviving the cold?" he asked.

"Just barely," Trixie said, feeling her cheeks start to tingle as the warm air hit them.

"We're fired up about the pet show, anyway. That helps," Honey told him.

"Ah, yes, the pet show." Nick reached under the counter and drew out a cardboard box and a thin catalog. "Ribbons first." He opened the box and drew out ribbons in purple, blue, red, and yellow. Some of the ribbons were plain, and some had rosettes on the top. "You told me everyone's to be a winner at this show, so I wasn't sure you'd want a different color for first-, second-, and third-place. Still, all blues or purples could be boring."

"Hmm. Good point." Trixie considered the ribbons that were lying on the counter.

"Every animal has its own category—or will, if Mart ever gets his computer program

running. So there can't be any second-places,"
Honey said.

Suddenly, Trixie had an idea. "Of course.
We need all first-place ribbons."

"They aren't really first-place, if there's only
one animal per category. They are all champi-
ons, though, so let's make all the ribbons purple," Nick said.

Trixie nodded emphatically. "Perfect solution."

"But still a little boring," Nick said. "Isn't
there some way to liven things up?"

"Not without getting Dr. Chang into trouble
with the pet owners," Honey said. "We can't
risk that. He agreed to judge only because we
promised to have a prize for every pet."

"Wait a minute!" Trixie said. "What about a
'People's Choice Award'? Everyone who buys
a ticket can get a ballot, and *they* can vote for
their favorite pet. Then we'll have a special
award without putting Dr. Chang on the spot."

"Oh, Trixie, that's perfectly perfect!" Honey
exclaimed.

"It is, indeed," Nick said. He flipped
through the catalog. "Here's a trophy that
would work well. It's a simple loving cup on a
walnut base with a plaque that we can en-

grave: 'People's Choice Award, Sleepyside-on-the-Hudson Pet Show,' and the date. How does that sound?"

Trixie's shrug showed that she had nothing to add. "It's perfect!"

"Fine. I'll have everything ready by a week from Saturday," Nick said.

"Gleeps! That sounds so close!" Trixie exclaimed.

"It *is* close. And there's so much more to do!" Honey added.

"That means we'd better get going," Trixie told Nick. The girls pulled on their hats, jackets, and mittens, and hurried back outside.

"That didn't take long at all," Trixie said as they headed down the street. "There's plenty of time for a stop at the World Anti-Hunger Foundation."

"You aren't going to just walk in and accuse Paul Gale of starting the rumor, are you?" Honey asked worriedly.

"Of course not. How unsubtle do you think I am? I'll just try to get him talking and see if he says anything suspicious."

The trouble was, Trixie didn't have the slightest idea what she'd say to Paul Gale. She lapsed into silence as she planned the conversation in her mind. Lost in this imaginary dialogue, she was surprised to look up and see the foundation office up ahead. The sight of someone in heavy winter clothes coming out of the office added to her surprise.

*It's Norma Nelson, it has to be*, Trixie thought. *I'd know that clumsy walk of hers anywhere, wouldn't I?* Trixie stared hard at the person, who was moving away from her, trying to decide if her eyes could possibly be deceiving her. *What would Norma be doing here? She should be out on her route on Glen Road this time of day. Why would she be visiting Paul Gale?*

Just as Trixie opened her mouth to ask Honey if she'd noticed too, the person disappeared around the corner. *Well, it just couldn't have been Norma, that's all*, she thought. *Meantime, here we are at the foundation office, and I haven't decided what I'm going to say to Paul Gale.*

As it turned out, however, Trixie didn't have to say anything to Paul Gale, because he wasn't in his office. Instead, a young blonde woman, simply dressed in a woolen skirt and matching sweater, came out of a back room and greeted the girls. "Welcome to the World Anti-Hunger Foundation," she said. "Have you come to make a pledge to help us in our work?"

"N-no," Trixie said, taken aback. *What should I say I'm here for?* she thought frantically.

"We just came in to find out more about the foundation," Honey said smoothly. "We saw Paul Gale on television the other day."

The young woman smiled. "Hearing Paul's message inspires many people to give. That's why he spends so much time away from the office, getting that message across to as many people as possible. Meantime, I'd be happy to tell you about the foundation."

She walked across the room to a large map of the world that was pinned on the wall. "The red pins on the map indicate all of the areas where desperately poor and needy people are receiving food and emergency supplies from the foundation," she said, pointing to the map.

"The green pins," she continued, "indicate all those cities and towns in the United States where people are contributing money to the foundation."

Trixie noted that the number of green pins far outnumbered the red ones, and she mentioned that fact out loud.

"Of course," the young woman said. "The

ratio of donors to recipients has to be five or six to one. For example, your pledge won't be enough to entirely support a needy person."

Trixie began to feel a slightly choked feeling, as if the woman were exerting a physical pressure on her.

The woman led the girls across the room to a huge leather photo album that was lying open on a lectern. "Here are some pictures of people who have been helped by contributions like yours," she said.

Over the woman's bent head, Trixie darted a look at Honey. Honey rolled her eyes in a "can you believe it?" expression. She was no more impressed by the woman's high-pressure tactics than Trixie was.

The pressure stayed on as the girls gradually extricated themselves from the office. The woman asked them outright for a contribution, and then for their names and addresses so that they could be added to the mailing list. When those requests were refused, she finally resorted to thrusting contribution envelopes into their hands. "Just mail us your pledge whenever you're ready to make the commitment," she said.

Trixie and Honey, having backed themselves to the door, turned and escaped through it.

"Wow!" Trixie said when she was safely back out on the sidewalk. "That was awful! I've seen barkers at the carnival who didn't sell as hard as that woman!"

"Trixie—" Honey began in a voice that sounded vaguely alarmed.

"Oh, I know. It is a charity, and they are raising money for a good cause, but I still don't think they have to behave that way. After all—"

"Trixie!" Honey's tone was escalating.

"All right, all right! I won't criticize them anymore. But from the way you looked in there, I didn't think you appreciated that woman's sales pitch any more than I did!"

"I didn't. And that *wasn't* why I was trying to get your attention just now. I wanted to tell you that the nice man who gave us the forty-dollar donation at the mall is sitting in a parked car right across the street."

Trixie quickly looked up and turned her head. Out of the corner of her eye she could see a parked car, but she had already walked well past it. There was no way for her to see the driver. "Oh, woe, I missed him because I was ranting on about the foundation. Are you sure it was him?"

"Absolutely," Honey said. "In fact, I noticed him sitting there when we were on our way into the office. I wasn't really sure then, so I didn't say anything. But I took an extra-close look when we came out. Now I'm sure."

"Let's turn around and go back, so I can get a look at him."

"We don't want him to notice we've seen him, though."

"Why not? We have every right to be here. We aren't doing anything wrong. And he shouldn't mind being noticed, unless—" Trixie broke off, her blue eyes widening.

"Do you suppose *he's* doing something wrong?" Honey asked, picking up on her friend's thought.

"He was right behind Paul Gale at the mall," Trixie said. "Now he's right outside Paul Gale's office. Maybe—maybe he's planning to rob the foundation! They must take in tons of money."

"Maybe," Honey said reluctantly. "But he didn't seem like a robber to me. Maybe he's Paul Gale's bodyguard."

Trixie snorted at the idea. "He's hardly any

bigger around than I am! Some bodyguard. Besides, he didn't seem to like Paul Gale. That's why he gave us all that money. He wouldn't work for him!"

"I guess not," Honey said.

Trixie walked on silently for a while, trying to pull another theory out of the cold air. Nothing came to her.

"What should we do?" Honey asked.

"Just head back to the school, I guess," Trixie said.

She was distracted by a gasp from Honey. "Look at the clock there on Nordin's jewelry store," Honey said. "We have exactly two minutes to get back to school and get our ride home with the boys!"

"Oh, no! They probably wouldn't leave us behind if we're late. But they'd chain us to that sign-up table, for sure. Let's hurry before we're trapped!" As Trixie spoke, she broke into a fast walk. Honey hurried to keep up.

The mystery of the nice man from the mall was left behind—but not forgotten.

# 8 * Dressed for Waiting

THE MYSTERIOUS RUMOR, the aggressive woman at the World Anti-Hunger Foundation, Paul Gale, and the nice man from the mall were very much on Trixie's mind that evening—much more so than the French Revolution, which was the subject of the chapter she was supposed to be reading for her world history class. Only her brothers' heavy concentration, as they sat in the den with her, made her try to keep her mind on her textbook.

A peculiar noise from Mart—a combination

of a groan and a growl—made her look up. "What is it? What's wrong?" she asked, eager for a momentary distraction.

"A mere comment on the complexity of computers," Mart said loftily.

"Are you still having problems?" Trixie asked.

"There are problems, but I have no doubt that I'll be able to correct them," Mart said confidently.

"How do you know where to find them?" Trixie asked, closing her textbook as she got up and moved over to the chair in which her brother was sprawled.

"The computer, in its vast wisdom, tells me where they are." Mart produced a sheaf of printout paper and handed it to his sister.

Trixie began to read it aloud. " 'Caution—word is not set above. Fatal—missing end statement. Caution—incorrect argument type. Warning—substring constant outside bounds.' Gleeps, are all of these 'cautions' and 'warnings' and 'fatals' errors in the program?" Trixie asked.

"Errors or potential errors. One simply corrects them or ignores them. Unfortunately," Mart added, "another error seems to crop up to take the place of each corrected one." It seemed to Trixie that a slight frown had replaced Mart's usually confident look.

"But will it finally work?" Trixie asked. "The pet show is less than a week and a half away!"

"The program will be functioning by then, I assure you." Mart spoke calmly, but he took the program out of Trixie's hands with a little more energy than was necessary.

Trixie rose and walked slowly back to the chair she'd abandoned along with her attempts at studying. She had just settled in when the phone rang. She jumped to her feet again. "I'll get it!" she called.

When she answered the phone, she was surprised to hear Nick's voice. "How's everything going?" he asked.

"Fine," Trixie said. "How's everything with you?"

There was a slight hesitation before Nick spoke again. "I'm fine, too. But, um, has something gone wrong with the pet show?"

Trixie felt a cold clutch of fear in her stomach. "N-no. Not that I know of. Why?"

"Well, I had the radio on while I was studying just now, and the announcer on WSTH said that the pet show had been canceled. But I guess I just misunderstood, since you didn't say you called it off."

"The show is on—but maybe you *did* hear it was canceled," Trixie said.

"I don't understand," Nick told her.

"I don't, either. But I'm going to find out. Thanks for calling, Nick." Trixie said good-bye quickly, hung up the phone, and hurried into the den. "Nick Roberts just heard on the radio that the pet show has been canceled," she told her brothers.

"Canceled?" Brian said. "Who'd do a thing like that?"

"I don't know," Trixie said grimly, "but I intend to find out."

She was on her way back to the telephone when it rang again. This time when she answered it, she heard Honey Wheeler's distraught voice: "Trixie, the most awful thing has happened!"

"You heard the announcement on the radio," Trixie guessed.

"Did you hear it, too?" Honey asked.

"I didn't. Nick Roberts did, and he called to tell me about it. It's another act of sabotage, Honey. I'm sure of it."

"What will we do?" Honey wailed.

"First, I'll call the radio station and let them know the show isn't canceled. Then I'll try to find out who started this," Trixie said.

"I'll let you go, then. Let me know what happens," Honey said as she hung up.

Trixie looked up the telephone number for the radio station with trembling hands. She dialed the number, and the announcer himself answered.

"My name is Trixie Belden," she told him. "You just announced that a pet show I'm helping with has been canceled. That information is wrong. Could you tell me where you heard it?"

"Why, from you," the announcer said. "Or someone who claimed to be Trixie Belden. But the voice was nothing like yours. I'm sorry if there's been a misunderstanding."

*There's that word again*, Trixie thought. *But this is more serious than a simple misunderstanding.* Aloud she only said, "The pet show hasn't been canceled. It's important to us that everybody knows that."

"Of course. I'll make the announcement several times tonight. I'll make sure the morning announcer mentions it, too. I'm sure there will be no permanent harm done from this."

*I hope not*, Trixie thought uneasily. She thanked the announcer and hung up.

"What happened, Trix?" Brian asked. "Did you get it all straightened out?"

Trixie told her brothers about the announcer's call from the imposter, and about his promise to set the record straight.

"That was a close one," Mart said. "It's lucky we caught it when we did, so there's no harm done."

"Maybe next time we won't be so lucky," Trixie muttered.

"Let's hope there won't be a next time," Brian said.

"What if just hoping isn't enough?" Trixie challenged him. "I think we should be *doing* something to stop the sabotage."

"Like what?" Brian asked. "We have no suspects, and no idea what the motive is behind the acts of sabotage. We don't even know that it *is* sabotage."

"Oh, come on!" Trixie said impatiently.

Brian raised his hand to fend off Trixie's protest. "All right, the rumor and the cancellation announcement are suspicious. But how can we prove anything?"

"The proof has to be somewhere," Trixie said stubbornly.

"Maybe," Brian acknowledged. "But finding it would take too much time and energy, and we don't have enough of either one."

"That is a reiteration of a reasonable rationale," Mart added.

Realizing that there was no point in arguing with her brothers, Trixie went back to the telephone, this time to call Honey Wheeler.

"Is everything straightened out?" Honey asked as soon as she picked up the phone.

"Well, the show is *un*canceled. But we have to figure out who's responsible for the sabotage, Honey. Otherwise—" Trixie let the unspoken threat hang in the air.

"I don't even know where to start," Honey said hopelessly.

"I do—with Paul Gale."

"You think *he* called the radio station and pretended to be you?" Honey asked, totally baffled.

"I don't think *he* did, but he could have asked his assistant to make the call."

"Have you told Brian and Mart about your suspicions?"

"They'd just laugh at me. And this is no

laughing matter."

"But what can we do? The boys won't believe us without more proof, and nobody else
will believe us if they don't."

"We'll have to get more proof, then."

"But how? Do you have a plan?"

Just as Honey asked the question, an idea
came to Trixie's mind. It was far from fool-
proof, she realized; it was also far from comfortable, but— "There's something we can
try," Trixie said. "It just might work. Bring ex-
tra-warm clothes to school tomorrow, and tell
your parents you'll be home late."

"But what—"

"I can't tell you more right now, because I
don't *know* any more. I'll have it all figured
out by tomorrow. See you then." Trixie hung
up before Honey could ask for more information.

The next afternoon, the girls told their
brothers they'd be taking the second bus
home. "We have an errand to run in town,"
Trixie said vaguely.

Then they ducked into the washroom to
pull on the extra sweatshirts and tights they'd
brought along that morning.

"I can hardly *move*," Honey said as she zipped up her jacket over four layers of clothes.

"Well, you aren't dressed for moving. You're dressed for waiting."

"Waiting for what?"

Trixie, enjoying the suspense but also concerned about her plan, only answered, "You'll see."

The two girls left the school and retraced their steps to the World Anti-Hunger Foundation office. The alley next to the building was narrower than Trixie had remembered. It had a high fence at the back. "Get in there, out of sight," she told Honey. She darted in behind her friend just long enough to open her book bag and get out a rolled-up poster announcing the pet show, a small package of thumbtacks, and a hammer.

Honey watched, wide-eyed, but didn't ask any more questions. Trixie didn't offer any more information, either, until after she had darted out of the little alley, tacked the poster up on a telephone pole outside the foundation office, and ducked back into the alley again.

"Now we wait for Paul Gale to see the poster," Trixie said.

"Then what?" Honey asked, already stomping her feet as the cold air began to nip at them.

"We see how he reacts," Trixie said. "Remember that time I'd suspected Nick Roberts of sabotaging one of our events because I saw him tear a flier off the wall at school? Well, I started thinking that if Paul Gale hates the pet show as much as we think he does, he'd probably react pretty violently if he saw a poster for it."

"So if Paul Gale comes along and rips down our poster, it means he's the saboteur?" Honey said skeptically.

"Of course not," said Trixie. "It just means he's worth keeping an eye on. Maybe we can even convince Jim and Brian and Mart of that fact."

Honey sniffed, but it was from the biting cold, not in response to Trixie's statement. "We have no idea how long it might take Paul Gale to come along and see the poster, though, do we?"

Trixie shook her head. "That's why I said to wear warm clothes."

The girls' conversation stopped for a while. They concentrated on watching the telephone pole, and on keeping warm. The second task proved impossible. Within minutes, Trixie's feet had begun to ache from the cold. Stamping them to warm them only produced more pain. Then her nose began to tingle, and she covered it with a mittened hand. But the moisture from her breath soon made the mitten damp. She knew that wet cold could cause more trouble than dry cold, so she lowered her hand. The cold air slapped her in the face like a giant fist.

She glanced over at her best friend. Although Honey was no longer as delicate as she once had been, her naturally slender frame gave her very little protection against the cold. Honey's eyes were bright with standing tears, and her cheeks were crimson.

*We aren't going to be able to stay out here very long,* Trixie thought. *This idea is too risky to be worth getting sick over.*

Just then, the girls heard footsteps on the sidewalk. Trixie drew farther back into the alley, to be sure that her shadow couldn't be seen on the walk. Then, carefully, she edged forward again until she could see around the corner of the building.

What she saw made her gasp.

"What is it?" Honey whispered.

"Somebody's standing right in front of the phone pole, reading the poster," Trixie said.

"Is it Paul Gale?" Honey asked.

"I can't tell. All I can see is his back. He's reaching toward the poster. He's—"

The ripping noise told Honey all she needed to know. "He tore it down, didn't he?"

Trixie nodded excitedly. "He did! He—uh-oh. Honey, duck back. He's heading this way!"

Honey scrambled backward, pressing against the wall of the building. Trixie moved back next to her.

The two girls waited in silence as the footsteps drew near. Trixie found herself holding her breath.

Then they felt a sudden gloom as a shadow fell across the little alley where they were standing. The man was coming closer. . . .

Poster still in hand, the man was soon standing right in front of the alley, staring at Trixie and Honey, blocking their way out.

# 9 ∗ The End of a Suspect

"I BELIEVE this belongs to you," the man said, holding the poster out to Trixie and Honey.

Trixie recognized the nice man from Sleepyside Mall. There seemed to be an amused twinkle in his eyes. "I put it on the telephone pole," she told him. Instinctively, she knew she had nothing to fear from him, but the fear she'd felt before she recognized him still hadn't completely gone away.

"Would you mind telling me why?" he asked. He continued to hold the poster out to the girls. With its bright yellow paper and bold black lettering, it seemed to demand an explanation.

"We're trying to get people to come to the pet show," Honey said bravely. "The posters are good publicity."

"Do you specifically need to have Paul Gale in attendance?" the man said in a sarcastic but gentle voice.

Trixie felt a momentary whirl of confusion. How would she explain her suspicious behavior? Then she thought reasonably, *I don't have to explain—at least, not until this man does. After all, he's been behaving as strangely as we have!*

Lifting her chin in a show of confidence she didn't really feel, Trixie asked, "Could you get Paul Gale to come to the show? You seem to be pretty close to him—after all, being parked across the street is pretty close. . . ."

The man's eyes darkened in a look that could have been either fear or anger. For a moment, Trixie felt another surge of nervousness. *Here I am, trapped between two buildings by a man whose name I don't even know, and I'm telling him he's been acting suspiciously. Dumb, Trixie, really dumb.*

But the man's agitated look was quickly replaced by the calm mildness that Trixie had seen before and instinctively trusted. "You're very observant," he said.

"I—" Trixie started to say that Honey had been the one to notice the occupant of the parked car. But she realized that she might be letting her friend in for danger, not praise. "I saw your car over there once, yesterday afternoon," she concluded lamely.

"Mmmm." The man quickly changed the subject. "It certainly is cold out here," he said. "You two girls must be nearly frozen."

"We are," Honey admitted.

"There's a nice little cafe around the corner," the man said. "Why don't the three of us go over there and have something warm to drink while we continue our little chat."

Trixie took a closer look at him. *There can't be any danger in drinking hot chocolate with him*, she thought.

Just as she was about to voice her agreement, Honey spoke up. "I'll have hot chocolate with *four* marshmallows."

The man laughed his low, hearty laugh. Trixie once again felt assured that she had nothing to fear from him. "Off we go, then," he said, standing back from the alley and gesturing the two girls out ahead of him. "By the way," he said, with a tip of his hat, "my name is David Llewelyn."

Trixie and Honey introduced themselves, then tucked their hands into their pockets and their chins into their collars for the walk to the cafe.

The silence lingered for a few seconds after the three of them were settled on the springy, vinyl-covered seats of a back booth. Trixie and Honey clutched their thick white mugs in both hands, enjoying the warmth. David Llewelyn made small circles with his coffee cup on the scratched and scarred wood table.

Soon Trixie began to feel nervous again. The only cure, she knew, was to end the silence. "So. Are you one of Paul Gale's followers?" she asked.

David Llewelyn looked up, slightly startled. Then his eyes took on their amused twinkle once again. "In a manner of speaking, I suppose I am. But I believe I was the first to ask for an explanation, back there by the foundation office. So I think you should be the first to give one."

Trixie hesitated, but Honey seemed to have warmed to David Llewelyn. "We think he might be trying to sabotage the pet show," she said. Quickly, she sketched in the details— Gale's criticism of the show on television, the rumor, and the cancellation announcement on the radio. As she spoke, she seemed to realize how sketchy the details were; how thin the thread was that linked Paul Gale to the sabotage. "We aren't ready to accuse him of anything, of course," she added. "That's why we put up the poster and waited for his reaction to it. We need more proof that he's our man."

David Llewelyn listened to Honey with an expression of calm seriousness. When she had finished, however, he shook his head. "I don't think the sabotage is the kind of thing Paul Gale would do."

"I know it seems strange, when he has such a reputation for good deeds, but—" Honey's defense of their suspicion was cut short by a gesture of David Llewelyn's upraised hand.

"That isn't why I doubt your theory," he said. "I am not blinded by the bright light of Paul Gale's reputation, believe me. Nonetheless, I am not willing to believe that he has been actively sabotaging your pet show. That simply doesn't fit in with—"

The half-sentence lingered in the air. David

Llewelyn busied himself with pouring another cup of coffee from the carafe, adding a precise measure of cream, and stirring slowly and carefully.

Eventually, it became obvious that he had no intention of finishing the sentence—at least, not voluntarily.

"Doesn't fit in with what?" Trixie asked bluntly.

David Llewelyn lifted his spoon out of the cup and shook it gently. He set it on the saucer. Then he picked up the cup and held it, seeming to weigh it. Finally he took a sip, set the cup down, and asked, "Can you girls keep a secret?"

Trixie felt a thump of excitement in her chest. "You bet," she said.

"Of course we can," Honey said.

David Llewelyn shook his head again. "I believe that you mean what you say, but I don't know if you understand how important this particular secret is. You can't confide in another friend or your parents or a favorite teacher—nobody."

"We know about secrets," Trixie said sternly.

The look of confidence in her eyes seemed

to convince David Llewelyn. He folded his hands on the table and began to talk. "The idea of Paul Gale sabotaging your pet show doesn't fit in with what I've learned about him as a special investigator assigned to his case for the past six months," he said.

Trixie was breathless for a moment as the words sank in. She felt Honey shift excitedly on the seat next to her.

David Llewelyn seemed purposely to have made his most startling announcement first. When he spoke again, it was in a more leisurely way. "I'm employed by the state Attorney General's office," he said. "I have been an investigator for nearly twenty-five years. My specialty is large-scale consumer fraud cases. That means someone is cheating the public out of thousands and thousands of dollars.

"As I said, I've been assigned to the Paul Gale case for the past six months. We have reasons for believing that the World Anti-Hunger Foundation is not entirely on the level. We have no proof—a dilemma you girls apparently understand. My job is to find some."

"Do you mean that Paul Gale keeps the money for himself, instead of feeding the poor with it?" Honey asked, sounding shocked.

"In fact, what we suspect is worse than

that," David Llewelyn said. "He does take the money to poor countries. Apparently he even buys some food with it, so that his operation looks legitimate. But we think he spends most of the money on gems—rubies, diamonds, emeralds—which he smuggles back into this country and sells for a fortune."

Trixie realized that her mouth had fallen open as she listened. She closed it and swallowed hard to moisten her dry throat.

"You can see why I was reluctant to tell you all this. I would be in serious trouble if you told anyone else. Worse, the entire investigation could be in jeopardy if word got out that Paul Gale is under suspicion. But I think it's important for you to know what kind of man we think Paul Gale is."

"But if he's capable of taking money away from the poor, why are you so sure he wouldn't sabotage our pet show?" Honey asked.

"For that very reason," David Llewelyn said. "The stakes that Paul Gale is playing with are huge. Literally millions of dollars by now, I'd say. He wouldn't risk that for a small-time pet show. No offense," he added quickly.

"Would he risk attacking the show publicly?" Trixie asked.

David Llewelyn waved a dismissing hand.

"There's no risk in that. Paul Gale has built the foundation on his image as an angry young man. That's what attracts people to him. Oddly enough, it's what makes people trust him. They like his zeal, and his willingness to speak up for what he believes—no matter what people might think of him for it. He's convinced his followers that he cares nothing for himself, but only for the poor.

"Attacking your pet show publicly—with words—would strengthen that image. It might be just the kind of thing he'd need to get himself established here in Sleepyside."

"But attacking the pet show with acts of sabotage could get him in trouble," Trixie concluded.

"Exactly. At the least, it might discourage his followers if he were caught harassing a group of teenagers. At most, it might bring him to the attention of the law. And I don't think he can afford that. Anyone who comes between Paul Gale and his millions will not have a pleasant fate awaiting him. I guarantee it."

There was such heaviness in David Llewelyn's usually pleasant voice that Trixie felt a shiver run up her spine. "It sounds as though we'd better stay away from Paul Gale," she said softly.

"I'm glad I made my point," David Llewelyn said, relieved. "It was well worth the cost of two cups of hot chocolate." He picked up the check the waitress had left on the table. "Now I'd best get back to work, and you'd best get back home."

Trixie nodded and slid out of the booth. "The thing is, we still don't know who's sabotaging our pet show."

The investigator hesitated on his way to the cashier. "That's right, you don't. Well, if there are any more problems, just call me at the Sleepyside Inn. We can get together and talk about the case."

"Really? Do you really mean it?" Trixie asked. Remembering all the times that Sergeant Molinson of the Sleepyside police department had shooed her away, the idea that a real investigator would discuss a case with her seemed almost too good to be true.

"Really," David Llewelyn promised. "After all, I took away your best suspect. The least I can do is help you find another one. But I sincerely hope that you won't encounter any more problems with your show."

# 10 ✳ A Last-Minute Entry

THERE WAS another pet show problem the very next day, however.

It was late Saturday afternoon, and Trixie had come home after the sign-up at the mall. She was in her room, studying world history. There was a soft knock at her door, followed by a loud thump. The combination of sounds was one Trixie had heard many times before. She sat up on her bed and groaned. "You can come in, Bobby," she said loudly. "Reddy has to wait outside."

"Okay," Bobby Belden shouted. Then, in a

softer voice, he added, "You wait here, Reddy. No, wait here. Wait! Reddy!" His young voice was becoming more and more impatient as he spoke. Soon it was drowned out by a series of thumps, yelps, and barks.

Trixie groaned again. "Oh, all right. Reddy can come in, too."

Immediately, the door burst open. Reddy bounded into the room, his head held high, his tongue lolling out of his mouth. Bobby followed his dog, seeming more restrained only because he was on two legs instead of four. Eventually the dog's excitement at being invited into Trixie's room began to wane, and he sat down next to Bobby, who was perched on Trixie's desk chair.

"Now," Trixie said, "to what do I owe this unexpected visit?"

Bobby didn't answer immediately. He stared at Reddy and patted the dog's neck.

"Bobby, honey, I want to help if I can. I need to study, though. So please, tell me what you want."

Bobby cleared his throat and looked up at his sister. "I want Reddy to be in the pet show next Saturday," he said simply.

Trixie sighed. "We can't let you do that,

Bobby," she said, deciding that a direct approach was best.

"Why not?" Bobby asked.

"We decided that, since the Bob-Whites are sponsoring the show, none of us can enter a pet."

"But I'm not a Bob-White," Bobby replied immediately. "You always say that I'm too young to be a Bob-White."

"You are," Trixie said firmly.

"Then why can't I enter Reddy in the pet show?" Bobby asked.

"Because Reddy's my dog, too, and *I'm* a Bob-White," Trixie said.

"You don't ever play with Reddy or take him for walks. You don't even feed him unless Moms tells you to," Bobby said accusingly.

"Reddy is really your dog, Bobby. You know that, and I know that. But other people think he belongs to all the Beldens. They'll see that Reddy is entered, and they'll think it's unfair. That's why we can't let you enter him in the show. Do you understand?"

Bobby was staring at the back of his dog's neck. His lower lip was thrust forward, and his cheeks were flushed.

*Oh, please don't let him cry,* Trixie thought.

But Bobby didn't start to cry. "Okay," he said with a strange firmness. "If I can't enter Reddy in the pet show because the Bob-Whites can't enter the pet show, then can I be a Bob-White?"

"That's blackmail!" Trixie shrieked.

"What does that mean?" Bobby asked, looking at his sister owlishly.

"Never mind," she said hurriedly. "Listen, this isn't a decision that I can make all by myself. The Bob-Whites make all of our really important decisions together. At our meeting tomorrow, I'll see what they think about the idea of your entering the pet show."

"Or becoming a Bob-White," Bobby added.

There was a predictable chorus of groans the next afternoon when Trixie opened the Bob-Whites' meeting by explaining Bobby's request.

"Well, we can't let Bobby become a Bob-White. That's simply out of the question," Honey said.

Jim shrugged. "I think we should let him enter the pet show. After all, we're only sponsoring the contest; we're not judging it. I don't see how we can be accused of playing favorites if Reddy wins something."

Trixie was convinced. "Okay, but our best protection is still that Reddy is too much of a harebrained hound to win anything."

"Oh, he'll win something," Jim said. "Remember, all the pets in the show will win awards."

"Speaking of winning . . ." Honey began. Tactfully, she didn't finish the sentence. Instead, she turned and looked at Mart.

"I know," Mart guessed. "You're wondering about my computer program. Don't worry. I expect to have the last few snags corrected by the end of class Monday morning."

"Hurray!" Honey shouted. "I have to confess, I was getting a little worried."

The Bob-Whites ended their meeting on that cheerful note, but the Beldens' happy mood was shattered when they returned to Crabapple Farm. The moment they entered the house, they could hear Bobby crying at the top of his lungs.

"What is it?" Trixie shouted. "What's wrong?" They raced upstairs to Bobby's room without even stopping to take off their coats.

Bobby was lying facedown on his bed. Mrs. Belden was sitting next to him, rubbing his back in a vain attempt to quiet his sobs.

Bobby looked up as his brothers and sister entered the room. "Reddy's gone," he wailed. "He's lost, and he's not ever going to come back."

"W-what?" Trixie looked at her mother, hoping that Helen Belden would have a less frightening explanation.

"Reddy and Bobby went out to play right after lunch. Reddy strayed off, and Bobby didn't notice until he was about to come back in. It didn't concern us at the time, but that was nearly four hours ago. That's a long time for Reddy to stay out in the cold."

"Oh, Bobby," Trixie said comfortingly, "that really isn't a *very* long time. Reddy will come back."

"Do you think so, Trixie?" Bobby asked, lifting his tear-streaked face from the pillow.

Trixie kneeled down beside him. "Sure, Bobby. We tease about how foolish Reddy is, but he's a smart dog, really. He'll find his way home."

"But when, Trixie?" Bobby asked. "When will Reddy come home?"

"Before morning, for sure," Trixie said.

By the next morning, Trixie was sorry she'd made the promise to Bobby. There was still no sign of the Irish setter when Jim and Honey came by in the station wagon to pick the older Beldens up for school. Bobby was more upset than he had been the previous afternoon.

The Wheelers were horrified at the news of Reddy's disappearance. "It's not like Reddy to run away," Honey said.

"I don't think he ran away at all," Trixie said. "I think he was stolen."

"Oh, come on, Trix," Brian said. "Reddy is cute, but he's hardly a prize. Who'd want to steal him?"

"Whoever wants to stop the pet show," Trixie replied. "First there was that rumor, then the phone call. Now someone's stolen our dog as a way of telling us we should stop the show."

"Only a future detective would come up with an explanation like that," Mart said.

"Do you have a better one?" Trixie challenged.

Brian spoke up. "For Reddy's disappearance? Sure. A passing rabbit that needed chasing, or a neighbor who needed visiting. Old Brom might have put him up for the night, figuring it was too cold to send him home. He doesn't have a car or a telephone. My guess is that Reddy will be home this afternoon by the time we are."

"What about the rumor and the phone call?" Trixie asked. "Do you think Old Brom is responsible for those, too?"

Brian was starting to lose patience. "Of course not. I don't know who's responsible for those things. But it doesn't matter, because they're over and there was no harm done. I'm not going to waste time worrying about them. Neither should you."

Jim had pulled the station wagon into a space in the school parking lot as Brian spoke. Before the car had fully stopped moving, Trixie threw the door open and scrambled out of the car. Without a backward glance, she hurried toward the school.

"Trixie, wait up!" Honey called.

"Sometimes those boys make me so mad," Trixie growled as Honey caught up to her. "Brian saw how heartbroken Bobby was yesterday afternoon. How can he be so smug?"

"He *is* concerned about Bobby," Honey replied softly. "He just doesn't believe that Reddy was stolen, that's all."

"Well, I do, and *that's* all," Trixie said defiantly. She started rummaging through her purse. Eventually she held up a quarter that had been floating around at the bottom. "I'm going to call David Llewelyn." She headed for a pay phone, with Honey right behind.

Trixie left a message that she and Honey would be at the cafe after school that afternoon. "I'd like him to meet us there to discuss the problem we talked about before," she said. She listened as the operator repeated the message, thanked her, and hung up.

Trixie went through the rest of the day in a haze. She was distant and distracted during lunch. So was Mart, whose corrections during computer class that morning hadn't resulted in a working program.

"I got permission to take a computer home tonight," he said. "I thought you wouldn't mind, Jim, since we have the station wagon anyway."

Jim made a carefree gesture with the hand that held his sandwich. "It will be a little crowded with seven people and one computer, but that's no problem," he said.

"Honey and I can minimize the crowding by taking the bus home," Trixie said quickly.

"You don't have to," Jim said.

"No—but we don't mind, either," Honey said quickly.

"See? That solves the problem," Jim told Mart.

*It certainly does*, Trixie thought with relief. Somehow, Trixie and Honey made it through the afternoon and finally found themselves at the cafe, waiting for David Llewelyn. The polite man didn't keep them waiting long.

"You say there's another problem?" he asked, frowning with concern, as he slid into the booth.

Trixie nodded and, without hesitation, told him about her dog's disappearance and her brother's unhappiness.

"Poor little boy," David Llewelyn said. "That's a problem, all right. Do you really think it's related to the other two, though?"

"I really do," Trixie said. "Reddy is one spoiled dog. He wouldn't stray far from home in this weather on his own."

"And you think Paul Gale is behind all three incidents?" the investigator asked.

"I don't know," Trixie replied. "You did a good job of convincing me he couldn't have been, and yet—"

"And yet," David Llewelyn repeated. "I know. You did a fairly good job of convincing me, too."

"You mean you think Paul Gale *is* involved?" Trixie asked excitedly.

"No, only that I'm less sure he isn't. It may be, strange as it sounds, that Paul Gale has some aversion to this pet show. In his greed, he may be seeing it as depriving him of donations that would otherwise be his." David Llewelyn shook his head. "This theory doesn't sound very logical, but six months of logic haven't helped on this case."

"It takes a lot more proof to convince people of something that sounds illogical," Trixie said, speaking from bitter experience. "And there's no way to prove that Paul Gale hates the pet show."

"Actually, there is," David Llewelyn said. "Now I don't want you to rush into this. I thought long and hard about even suggesting it to you."

"What?" Trixie asked. "What is it?"

"Well, we could wire you—send you into the foundation office carrying a concealed microphone. You could strike up a conversation with Gale. If he says anything that's remotely like a confession, I'd hear it—and I'd record it to use against him."

"Let's do it!" Trixie exclaimed.

"Now, wait—think about the risks. If he does have some sort of hatred for you and your pet show, this incident would only make it worse. If he explodes on the spot, I can come to your rescue. But if he keeps his cool, then starts stalking you later, there won't be much I can do."

"S-stalking?" Trixie repeated. It was an ominous-sounding word. She cleared her throat. "I don't care. If it gives us proof that Paul Gale is our saboteur, it's worth it. Go ahead and wire me."

"Then wire me, too," Honey said. "I'm not letting Trixie do this alone."

David Llewelyn smiled gently. "You don't need two microphones. But the moral support will be most welcome, I'm sure." He reached into his pocket and pulled out the microphone. It was tiny, no larger than the metal piece at the eraser end of a pencil. There was a clip on the back, which Llewelyn attached to the collar of Trixie's turtleneck sweater. "Leave your coat unbuttoned, and the collar will conceal the mike," he said.

"That's it? That's all? I'm ready to go?" Trixie asked.

David Llewelyn nodded. "Just turn and

look back before you go into the foundation office. By that time, I'll have taken a reading to make sure everything is working. If not, I'll signal you to come back."

Trixie nodded and looked at Honey. "Let's go," she said. The two girls left the booth, with David Llewelyn trailing a safe distance behind. When they got to their destination, the girls turned around and looked back. David Llewelyn was pretending to look at some merchandise in a store window.

"Should we wait here until he gives us a signal that everything is all right?" Honey asked.

"That *is* the signal," Trixie told her. She pushed open the door to the building and walked inside.

There was no sign of the young blonde woman who had been in the office before. Instead, the girls were greeted by Paul Gale himself. "Good afternoon," he said. "Welcome to the World Anti-Hunger Foundation. Would you like to know about the work we do here?"

"Yes, we would," Trixie said. "You see, we like to raise money for good causes, and we thought we'd do some work for the Anti-Hunger Foundation."

Paul Gale's eyes lit up. "That's wonderful!"

he said. "We especially appreciate help from young people."

"Good. I'm sure we'll enjoy helping," Trixie said. "Except—" She paused and drew a deep breath to steady her nerves. "Except we can't start quite yet. Right now, we're working on a pet show to raise money to save the game birds that are dying this winter."

The light went out of Paul Gale's eyes. "Of course, I should have recognized you from the Sleepyside Mall," he said with a smirk. "Well, I'm glad I got you to realize that feeding the game birds is a waste of time. I don't blame you for wanting to finish what you've already started, of course. But I'm glad you've decided to do something really worthwhile."

Trixie felt herself growing red with anger. She wanted to scream, *At least we're helping something besides ourselves and a bunch of black-market gem dealers!* Only the knowledge of David Llewelyn's need for secrecy made her bite her tongue.

"We're always interested in doing something worthwhile." Honey's voice was overly sweet. "I'm sure you'll realize that more and more as time goes on."

*Oh, wonderful, wonderful Honey,* Trixie

thought. *She's taking out her anger on Paul Gale, and he doesn't even know it.*

Indeed, Paul Gale didn't have a clue that Honey was being sarcastic. "I'm sure I will," he said with a smile. His heavy beard hid most of his face, so that the smile was really only a baring of teeth.

*Like a hungry animal,* Trixie thought.

Paul Gale launched immediately into roughly the same lecture his assistant had given the day before. The girls listened to it with jaws clenched. Trixie grew angrier and angrier at every claim of good works she heard Paul Gale make. Honey's tones grew sweeter and more admiring as she, too, became more irritated.

Finally the girls were able to disentangle themselves and head for the door. Outside, Trixie muttered a low growl and marched away from the building at a brisk pace.

"You were supposed to make Paul Gale angry," David Llewelyn said as he appeared from nowhere and fell in step beside the girls. "You weren't supposed to get angry yourself."

Trixie laughed in embarrassment. "I did, though. I got absolutely furious. I'm even angrier that nothing got accomplished in there."

"Oh, I wouldn't say that," David Llewelyn said as he reached out and unclipped the microphone from Trixie's collar. "After six months of trailing Paul Gale, I was getting discouraged. Hearing that smooth pitch of his made *me* angry, too—angry enough to tail him for another six months, if necessary."

"I hope it won't be," Trixie said. "If there's anything more we can do to help, just let me know."

"Thank you," David Llewelyn said. "But you'd better spend your time thinking about your own mystery."

# 11 * Computerized Confrontation

AS IT TURNED OUT, however, Trixie had very little time for thought that evening. She was just taking off her coat when Bobby ran to her. He wasn't crying, but his eyes were puffy and red-rimmed.

Trixie gave her younger brother a hug. "No sign of Reddy?" she asked softly.

The question was all it took to make Bobby start crying again. "N-no Reddy," he wailed. "Moms and me looked and looked this afternoon. She said you guys would help me look tonight. But Mart's gotta work on his computer, and Brian's gotta run an errand for Daddy. So would you help me look? Please?"

"Of course I will," Trixie told him without hesitation.

The two Beldens searched the grounds around Crabapple Farm until their feet were numb with cold. They shouted until their voices were hoarse. But there was still no sign of Reddy. Finally, concerned about the effect of the cold on Bobby, Trixie persuaded the unhappy six-year-old to go back inside.

"Brian and I will go out again after dinner," Trixie promised.

Dinner that night was a gloomy affair, very different from the usual noisy, enthusiastic occasion that the Beldens all enjoyed. Bobby only played with his food. Mart, usually the most talkative in the family, hardly said a word. He arrived at the table at the very last minute, quickly downed two helpings of roast beef and mashed potatoes, and asked to be excused to go back to his borrowed computer.

After dinner, Trixie helped her mother with the dishes while Brian went back outside to look for Reddy. Then Trixie joined her brother and the two of them made another round of the Belden property, calling Reddy's name.

There was no sign of the dog.

When Trixie and Brian came inside and admitted their defeat, Bobby's eyes once again filled with tears. "Come on," Trixie said, putting her arm around his shoulders and leading him upstairs. "I'll wash those tears off your face, and then I'll tell you all the stories I've heard about dogs who have been lost for days and weeks and months, even, and have found their way home."

"Really?" Bobby asked. "Is that true?"

"It's truly true," Trixie told him. *I just hope it turns out to be true for Reddy*, she thought.

Trixie didn't have to try to remember very many happy endings, however. The brisk exercise Bobby had put in during the day soon had him drifting off to sleep. Trixie kissed his cheek, which was ruddy and chapped from the cold air, and tiptoed out of his room, closing the door behind her.

As she passed Mart's room, she heard him say, in an exasperated voice, "I don't get this at all!"

Softly, Trixie walked into his room. "Your program still isn't working," she said sympathetically.

"It's working perfectly," Mart said. "That's

what I don't understand. I had such a confusing crazy quilt of corrections that I decided to go right back to the beginning. So I put the program in the same way I did two weeks ago at school, without any of the changes or modifications I've made since then—and now it works!"

"You must have done something differently, if it works now and didn't then," Trixie insisted.

"No, I put this exact same program in the computer," Mart said stubbornly. "It took me the whole hour. The next morning I came in and tried to run it, and—" Mart suddenly jumped to his feet, backing away from the computer as if it might be about to explode. "There's only one explanation. Somebody sabotaged my program after I left the computer room!"

Mart continued to stare at the computer. He stood with his feet wide apart, his shoulders pulled back, and his arms held stiffly out from his sides. It was, Trixie realized, the posture of a cowboy who was about to draw a six-gun and shoot down a villain.

That ridiculous thought snapped the tension that Trixie had been feeling all evening.

Suddenly, uncontrollably, she started to laugh.

Mart whirled and looked at her furiously. "What's so funny about someone sabotaging my program?" he demanded.

Somehow, Mart's rage made the whole thing seem even funnier. "N-nothing," Trixie said, her laughter contradicting the denial. "I'm sorry. It's been one of those days, I guess. But are you sure someone sabotaged the program?"

"How else do you explain it?" Mart asked. "This is the same program I typed into the computer two weeks ago. It works perfectly now, but it sure didn't then. That's why I've spent all this time trying to get the bugs out of it."

"But who would have done such a thing, and why?"

"I don't know why, but I do know who," Mart said grimly. "It would take a lot of knowledge about computers to ruin the program without my being able to spot the sabotage. There's only one person in my class who knows enough to do such a thing."

"Gordon Halvorson!" Trixie exclaimed.

"Gordon Halvorson," Mart confirmed.

"But why?" Trixie pressed. "I thought Gordon was so eager to teach you about computers."

"That's how he's been acting," Mart said. "But maybe he was being helpful as an excuse to hang around and make sure I *didn't* get the program working."

"Oh, but Mart, I can't imagine—" Trixie broke off as Brian Belden walked into the room.

"Still having problems with your program?" he asked.

"Not anymore," Mart said. "There's a different kind of problem now." Briefly, he told Brian what he'd concluded.

Brian let out a soft, low whistle. "So that's the story," he said. "Well, it's a relief. I was beginning to think you weren't as smart as you've been telling me you were."

"Terrific—another comedian," Mart said.

"This isn't funny, Brian Belden," Trixie said, forgetting that she had been laughing at Mart just a few minutes earlier. "Gordon deliberately sabotaged the program. What he did was wrong. Somebody has to make sure he doesn't try it again."

"You're right, Trixie. I apologize, Mart. I

guess I just wanted your programming problems to be over, so that we could concentrate full-time on the pet show and on finding Reddy. But you're right—Gordon has to be confronted."

Mart sank back down into his desk chair. He reached around to the back of the computer and pushed the off switch. The screen instantly went blank, but Mart continued to stare at it. "At least I've seen the last of that program," he said.

"The last of it?" Trixie shrieked. "Getting it working was just the beginning. Now you have to put all the data from all the pets into it."

Mart's jaw dropped open. He turned in his chair and stared dumbly at Trixie.

Again, Brian and Trixie began to laugh.

Mart wasn't amused. He rose, zombie-like, from his chair. "I'm going to bed," he announced.

"Sweet dreams," Trixie said in a syrupy voice. Then, bursting into laughter once again, she left her brother's room and headed for her own.

Alone in her room, however, Trixie found herself feeling far from cheerful. *Mart's pro-*

*gramming problems are over. But there are still so many other problems to be solved. I don't see how we can do it all before the pet show on Saturday.*

She fell into a worried sleep that was plagued by troubled dreams. In one dream, she was walking Reddy down Glen Road. The energetic setter suddenly lunged forward, wresting the leash from her hand. She called to him, but he was running after a boy. The boy turned around just as Reddy jumped at him, and Trixie saw the terrified face of Gordon Halvorson. Reddy knocked Gordon down, and Trixie ran forward to retrieve the dog and help Gordon to his feet. But by the time she got there, Gordon had turned into Paul Gale, and it was the man who was attacking the dog, rather than the other way around.

In her dream, Trixie cried out, but no one responded. She looked around frantically for help, and saw Norma Nelson standing silently by the side of the road.

"Help me, please," Trixie cried.

Norma's only response was to toss a handful of cracked corn into the air like confetti.

In the morning, Trixie woke feeling drained and tired. She straggled after her brothers out to the car, carrying Mart's book bag so that he could carry the computer.

At school, she followed Mart up to the computer room so that she could hand him his book bag as he dropped off the computer.

The computer room was large. There was a desk and chalkboard in the front of the room, with four rows of tables and chairs so that students could listen to lectures. The computers, on their special desks, were pushed up against the side and back walls.

Mart started toward an empty desk to put back his computer, then froze when he saw the lone student working at a computer in the far corner.

Trixie felt an urge to turn and run when she recognized Gordon Halvorson; she wondered briefly if Mart felt the same way. But it was too late. Gordon had heard them and turned around.

"Good morning," he said cheerfully, rising from his chair. He was a tall, thin boy with mud-colored hair that fell in a lifeless lock on his forehead. "Did you make any progress last night?"

"Yes," Mart said as he put down his computer.

"Well, good," Gordon said, not realizing

that anything was wrong. "We'll work on it this morning during class. Maybe we'll get those snags out for you."

"The snags are out," Mart said. For a moment, it seemed as though he would be unable to say anything more. Then, with great effort, he added, "I know what you've been doing, Gordon."

Gordon's face registered his shock vividly. His denial, when it came, was unconvincing: "I-I don't know what you mean."

"Yes, you do," Mart said. He seemed more at ease now that the initial accusation was over. "You've been sabotaging this program all the while you were pretending to help me with it. Last night, I tried the program as I'd originally written it two weeks ago, and it worked perfectly."

In spite of himself, Gordon looked impressed. "That was a smart way to handle it," he said. "I thought you'd just keep patching what you had. It never occurred to me that you'd try going back to the beginning."

*The nerve of him*, Trixie thought. *He's still acting superior, even now.* "Don't you think you've got some explaining to do?" she asked out loud.

Gordon shifted his attention to Trixie. "I

suppose I do. Well, primarily I made minor changes in the data base—the kind that no one would notice in a quick scan. From time to time, I also made some changes in the loops for each subsort, and—"

"But why?" Trixie demanded.

Gordon looked down, touching the keyboard of a computer, almost stroking the keys. "I just thought one of the Beldens could let someone else be good at something for a change."

Trixie looked at her brother to see if he'd understood Gordon's statement. When Mart shrugged, Trixie asked, "What does that mean, Gordon?"

Gordon looked up at Trixie. His mouth was set in an angry pout. "You Beldens and your rich friends—you're always hanging around in that tight little pack of yours, living in your own little world, working on your own little projects. You think you're too good for the rest of us. You think nobody has anything to offer you, because you've got it all."

"That's not true!" Trixie protested.

"Oh, yeah? Well, look what happened when I tried to help your brother learn about computers. He wouldn't have any of it; he just pushed me out of the way," Gordon said.

"I did not," Mart countered. "I was grateful for your help, but I couldn't learn just by watching you. I needed a chance to do things my own way and make my own mistakes. You wouldn't give me a chance."

"*I* wouldn't give *you* a chance? That sounds pretty funny, coming from you!" Gordon's lower lip suddenly started to tremble. He tried to control himself and, when he couldn't, he stormed out of the room.

Mart watched him go, looking pale and shaken. "I had no idea he felt that way," he said. "I could have listened to him a little more, if I'd known how important it was to him. Maybe then he wouldn't have had to—"

"To sabotage your program?" Trixie completed her brother's thought, but shook her head. "He didn't *have* to do that. And he was wrong to do it, although he doesn't seem to have admitted it. I don't think he should get away with it."

Mart sighed. "No. I'll have to tell the teacher."

"Do you want me to come along?" Trixie offered.

"No, I'd better do it alone."

Trixie held out Mart's book bag, feeling as though it were a shield she was offering before sending him out to do battle. "Good luck. I'll see you at lunch."

Mart was the last of the Bob-Whites to get to the cafeteria that noon. Trixie had filled the others in on what had happened, and they were all waiting eagerly for him.

"What happened? What happened?" Trixie asked as soon as Mart sat down.

He opened a carton of milk and took a long swallow before he replied. "Gordon admitted the sabotage in front of the teacher. Mr. Johnson was neat about it. He's not going to flunk Gordon, but he's going to make him spend a hundred hours doing programming for some charity project. They'll decide on one after school."

"That is a good solution," Honey said. "I guess the pet show project doesn't need him now, though, does it?"

"No, and I don't think that's a project he'd pick," Mart said. "You know, he never did say he was sorry. He's really convinced that we're a conceited little in-group."

"Do you think that a lot of people agree

with him?" Honey asked, sounding hurt.

"Not a lot, I'd guess," Jim told her. "I think it's more people like Gordon, whose lives aren't what they want them to be, and who need somebody to blame."

"Loneliness is so awful," Honey said. "It can make you think strange things sometimes. I know all about that."

"I wish we could do something to help Gordon," Di said.

"I do, too," Mart told her. "But I don't think he wants any help from the Bob-Whites right now."

"No, I'm sure he doesn't," Dan added.

"Well, we can't solve Gordon's problems, but I'm glad yours is solved, Mart," Brian said. "Now we can deal with the others—Bobby's lost dog and the endangered pet show."

"I wish we could solve those problems as easily," Jim said.

Something in their conversation had given Trixie an idea. "Maybe we can," she said quietly.

## 12 * Tailing a Suspect

"WHAT DID YOU SAY?" Brian asked.

"I—" Trixie began, then remembered the disbelief that had greeted all of her theories about the pet show. "There are some things that still need to be done before the pet show on Saturday," she said. "Honey and I had better stay in town after school and take care of them."

"What—" Honey started to question her friend's statement, then caught the warning arch of Trixie's eyebrow. "What a good thing that you remembered those details we talked about last night."

Only Jim caught the look that the two girls exchanged. *He knows there's something going on,* Trixie thought. *If he says anything to Brian and Mart, we won't be allowed out of their sight for the next month!*

To her surprise, however, Jim didn't voice his suspicions. He just gave Trixie a long, hard look. The look meant that Jim knew something suspicious was going on.

The warning bell sounded, ending the lunch hour. Trixie rose quickly and said, "See you tonight."

The Bob-Whites all gathered up the remains of their lunches as well as their books, and headed in different directions for their afternoon classes.

Trixie and Honey had only a moment together in the hallway after the others had left. "It's about Reddy, isn't it?" Honey asked her friend. "Are we going to find him this afternoon?"

"I hope so," Trixie said. "I have to get to class," she added. "Meet me at my locker after school."

The afternoon passed slowly for Trixie. At

last the bell rang, and she hurried to her locker. By the time she had put away her books and put on her coat, Honey was at her side.

"What are we going to do?" Honey asked eagerly.

"In detective terms, we're going to tail a suspect."

"Then you'd better start by telling me who the suspect is."

Trixie hesitated. Of course, she'd have to tell Honey whom she suspected. But once she did, her suspicions would be impossible to retract. She was letting herself wide open to look like a fool. Worse, she was opening the possibility of calling attention to an innocent person.

Finally, Trixie took a deep breath and spoke the name: "Norma Nelson."

"Norma!" Honey's voice somehow managed to combine a shout and a whisper. "You think she's been sabotaging the pet show?"

Trixie answered in a quick, hushed tone. "Before you tell me I'm crazy, just think about it for a minute. Norma has exactly the same reasons for sabotaging the pet show that Gordon had for sabotaging Mart's program. That's what made me think of her."

"She was the exclusive game-bird feeder until we came along, just as Gordon was the sole computer expert," Honey said.

"Exactly," Trixie said. "There are other similarities, too. She's been hovering around the pet show sign-up table just the way Gordon has been hovering around Mart during computer class. She hasn't been giving us advice, of course. But she's been keeping an eye on us just the same."

"So you think she started the rumor, called the radio station, *and* took Reddy—all to sabotage the show?" Honey asked. She sounded less than enthusiastic. "It sounds logical when you explain it, but I can't believe that quiet little Norma Nelson would do those things."

"Mart didn't suspect that Gordon Halvorson would sabotage his computer program, either, and look where it got him," Trixie said, no longer trying to keep the urgency out of her voice. "If Norma *is* the saboteur, and we don't do anything about it, we could wind up with a program and no pet show."

"I know," Honey said miserably. "But if we accuse her, and it turns out that she's innocent—Oh, Trixie, she's so shy. I don't know if she could stand something like that."

"If you'd rather not come along, I'll understand," Trixie said. "But I have to go now. I can't wait another day to find out if I'm right about Norma."

"Then let's go," Honey said decisively.

"All right! You take the side door, I'll take the front."

Trixie took off for the front door of the school. Once there, she waited on the steps outside.

Soon Norma came out and walked right past her. As quickly as she could, Trixie acted out a "remembering something" routine, raising her hand to her mouth and then sorting busily through her book bag before turning and walking swiftly back toward the side door.

"Let's go," she said to Honey.

The two girls walked quickly around to the front. Norma was still within easy view just ahead of them.

"You'll be gentle, won't you?" Honey asked. "I feel sorry for Norma."

"What about Bobby?" Trixie asked back. "Don't you feel a little sorry for him?"

"You know I do," Honey replied. "But even

though I know he misses Reddy horribly, I still don't think he's as lonely right now as Norma is every day of her life."

The girls followed Norma for several blocks. When Norma finally headed up the front walk of a pleasant, red-brick house, Trixie and Honey hurried to catch her.

"Norma!" Trixie shouted.

Norma turned and looked at the two approaching figures. She didn't speak, didn't move.

Very quickly, Trixie and Honey reached the spot where Norma stood waiting for them.

"I-I was just wondering if you've seen my dog," Trixie said. "He disappeared a couple of days ago. I know you spend a lot of time on Glen Road, and I thought you might have seen him."

Norma continued to stand and stare. For a moment Trixie thought she might not respond at all.

Finally Norma said, "I don't know anything about your dog. I don't even like dogs. I'm allergic to them."

At exactly that moment, a loud, deep bark resounded from inside the red-brick house.

Trixie and Honey turned toward the sound,

their attention momentarily diverted from Norma Nelson. When they turned back, a remarkable change had taken place in the girl. Her expressionless face had crumpled into a look of deep sadness.

"That's him," she wailed. "That's your dog. I'm sorry I took him. I'm really, really sorry."

"Could we go inside?" Honey asked softly. "We need to talk, and it's too cold to stand out here."

Norma nodded and took in a deep, shuddering breath. She led the way to the back door and opened it. "Mother!" she shouted. "Reddy's owner is here for him."

"At last!" Mrs. Nelson's voice sounded pleasant enough, but there was a lot of relief in her tone. "He's in the basement. You go right on down."

Reddy's barking increased as the girls walked down the stairs. When they entered the room, Reddy ran to Trixie, jumped up, and put his paws on her shoulders.

"Down!" Trixie shouted. She grasped his paws and pulled him free.

Reddy immediately went to Honey and jumped up to her. When Honey, too, forced him down, he simply ran through the basement in an aimless expression of joy.

*Only Reddy could make me so irritated at the same time that I'm so thrilled to see him,* Trixie thought with amusement.

"I've taken good care of him," Norma said. "But I can tell he belongs with you."

"Well, of course," Trixie said. "He's my dog!"

"I'm sorry I took him."

"What about the other things?" Trixie asked.

"I'm sorry about those, too."

"When did you decide to sabotage the pet show?" Honey asked.

"I didn't *decide* to wreck the pet show," Norma began. "One day in the lunch line, two girls ahead of me were talking about it. They were saying what a neat idea it was to save the game birds and how they were going to enter. It made me mad, because I'd been spending all my spare time feeding the game birds, and they were talking as if you guys had invented the idea. So I said, 'Are you sure that's how the Bob-Whites are going to spend the money?' They asked me what I meant. I said, 'They dress awfully well, in those fancy matching jackets. And they have two cars. I wonder where they got the money for all those things.'

"The girls looked surprised. One of them said, 'The Wheelers are rich. I heard Jim Frayne inherited money, too. They wouldn't need the money from the pet show.'

"That was that. I didn't say another word. But a couple of days later, I heard some other kids saying that the pet show is a big rip-off, and that the Bob-Whites are going to use the money they raise for clothes and cars.

"I was amazed," Norma continued. "I never wanted to start such a rumor. I just wanted to say something mean, I guess. But there it was, spreading all over the school. I felt like it was the first time anybody had ever listened to me."

"But we squelched the rumor by opening the bank account," Honey said softly. She was prompting Norma to continue talking.

"That's right," Norma said. "It was so easy for you to get everybody back on your side. I almost gave up. One day I didn't even go out to feed the birds. Let Trixie and her friends do it, I thought. But I missed the bird-feeding so much. I couldn't let you take it away from me.

"That—that's when I called the radio station." Norma swallowed hard. "It was scary to do that, but I had to because I was so angry."

"I still don't see why you were mad at us for trying to save the game birds," Trixie said. "You knew how badly they needed help."

Trixie and Honey were discovering the full range of emotions that lay buried under Norma Nelson's stoic exterior. They'd seen sadness, bitterness, and fear. Now they saw anger. "That just shows what you know, Trixie Belden!" she shouted. "You're so used to having everybody admire you and look up to you. What do you know about wanting to feel special and not ever being able to? What do you know about finding one thing that you think is important, and then having somebody else come along and do it so much bigger and better that you feel like a fool for doing it in your own silly little way?"

Trixie drew a deep breath. She knew she had to stay calm, but she also knew that she couldn't let Norma's statement go unchallenged. "We didn't make you feel like a fool, Norma. We only did what you yourself were trying to do—saving the birds. We even tried to get you involved, but you wouldn't listen to us. Maybe you were angry because you realized you were more concerned about yourself than about the birds.

"You know, Norma," Trixie said, pressing on

before her courage deserted her completely, "you said a few minutes ago that one of the things you don't like about the Bob-Whites is that we don't ask for help. But I'd say you're the one who's guilty of that."

"I see what you mean," Norma said quietly. "Maybe I haven't been putting the welfare of the birds first. Maybe I have been selfish."

"Stealing my dog was the worst of all," Trixie said softly.

Without warning, Norma's eyes brimmed with tears. "I didn't steal him—not really."

Trixie thought of a sarcastic response, but she bit it back before she spoke aloud. "What happened, then?" she asked.

"I was out feeding the birds along Glen Road when Reddy came running up to me. He was loose, and there was nobody around. I knew he was yours. His name was on his collar, and besides, I'd seen you with him.

"I grabbed him by the collar and started for your house, but then I got angry again. I thought about how much I want a dog, but my parents won't let me have one. And you have a beautiful dog that you don't even take care of. So I took him home."

"We *do* take care of him," Trixie said.

"There *was* somebody around that day—my six-year-old brother. That's really his dog you took home, and Bobby's been heartbroken ever since."

"I didn't know that," Norma said. Then she quickly held up a hand to stop the response that she knew would be coming from Trixie. "That's no excuse. I shouldn't have taken the dog. I wasn't going to keep him, though. I told my parents I'd put a notice up at school. I was going to tell them I'd heard from the owner right after—"

Norma stopped, but Honey intuitively finished the sentence. "Right after the pet show."

"That's right. I couldn't stop the show, but I could keep Trixie from winning it," Norma said. "I'm sorry. I'm glad none of the things I tried worked out. I didn't really do any damage, did I?"

"Of course not," Honey said, trying to make Norma feel better. "It would have been another story, though, if we'd pushed Paul Gale any harder when we thought he was—" Honey broke off suddenly and clapped her hand over her mouth.

Trixie pressed her own lips together, as if she could somehow block Honey's words.

Norma looked confusedly from one girl to the other. "Paul Gale?" she repeated. "Isn't he the man who gives all the food to poor people? What did you think he was?"

Honey looked at Trixie, and Trixie looked back at Honey. *It's a secret*, Trixie thought. *We aren't supposed to tell anyone, except that we already let on that there is a secret and—* "Oh, woe," she groaned. "We might as well tell you—but you have to promise not to tell anyone else."

Norma smiled a wry smile. "Who would I tell?" she asked.

*Well, what do you know? She even has a sense of humor*, Trixie thought. Briefly, she filled Norma in on her suspicions about Paul Gale and about the case that David Llewelyn was trying to build against him.

Norma sat listening as raptly as a youngster hearing a fairy tale. When Trixie had finished, Norma said in a husky whisper, "I think I overheard some evidence against Paul Gale."

Trixie and Honey stared at Norma in amazement. Then Trixie said, "Evidence? Against Paul Gale? He didn't sabotage the pet show; you did."

"The evidence isn't about the pet show,"

Norma said impatiently. "It's about the jewel smuggling and the foundation money and all that other stuff."

"Where did you hear it?" Honey asked.

"At the World Anti-Hunger Foundation," Norma said. "I went there one afternoon to talk to Paul Gale. I was angry about the pet show, but I didn't want him to make people stop feeding the birds, either. I went there to ask him not to make any more remarks about throwing money to the birds."

Trixie had begun to bounce up and down excitedly in her chair as Norma spoke. "I saw you!" she exclaimed. "You were coming out of the foundation office just as we were going in." Seeing Honey's surprised look, Trixie added, "I was going to point her out, but she turned the corner before I could."

"I was in a hurry," Norma said, "because I wanted to get home in time to feed the birds."

"You obviously didn't get to talk to Paul Gale, because if you were there the same day we were, Paul Gale wasn't around," Honey said. "His assistant was there alone."

"He was around," Norma said. "He was in the back room. His assistant was, too. When I walked into the office, there was nobody in the main room. The door to the back room was open, so I went over to it, thinking I'd just clear my throat to get someone's attention. I heard two people talking, though, so I decided to wait until they were finished with their conversation.

"First I heard a man's voice say, 'There sure are a lot of pigeons here in Sleepyside.' At the time, I thought he was talking about real pigeons. I was surprised at the remark— why would a stranger notice something like that about a town? Now, though, I think he meant—"

"Pigeons!" Trixie exclaimed. "Of course! That's what swindlers call their victims. He meant lots of people in Sleepyside are giving money to his phony foundation!"

Norma continued, ignoring the outburst. "Next, a woman's voice said, 'Well, it isn't pigeon feed that you'll be taking to Thailand next month.' I assumed she meant they were feeding people—not birds—because on TV he'd criticized feeding the birds. But—"

"But really that's the term swindlers use for a lot of cash," Trixie said. Realizing she'd interrupted again, she clapped her hand over her mouth.

Norma went right on. "Then, the man's voice said, 'Yeah, but it's a lot of ice I'll be bringing back.' Now that really confused me, because I always thought it was hot in Thailand, so you wouldn't think they'd be exporting ice. Besides, ice is so easy to make, I couldn't imagine anyone importing it, and—"

Trixie had to speak up or burst. "Ice! Gems! He was admitting he buys gems with the money!"

# 13 * The Evidence on Ice

"WE HAVE TO TELL David Llewelyn about this," Trixie told Norma. "Is there a phone down here?"

As soon as Norma pointed out the phone, Trixie bounded to her feet. Reddy, who had been waiting patiently, bounded up right with her.

In seconds, Trixie was back. "David Llewelyn isn't around," she said, "so I left a message. I can't wait to tell him about this!"

"Then let's not wait," Honey said. "I bet we can find him down by the foundation office."

"Good idea," Trixie said. "Except for one thing." She cast a pointed look at Reddy. "We can't take him downtown with us. He'd call attention to us *and* to David Llewelyn.

"Okay, here's what we'll do," Trixie continued. "You and Norma head downtown. Brian and Jim are at the sign-up table at school, so I'll drop Reddy off there. I'll tell the boys I have to meet you, so I can't stay."

"Will they buy that?" Honey asked.

"It doesn't matter," Trixie said. "Even if they take me home, you and Norma will still be able to get to David Llewelyn with the evidence against Paul Gale. Let's go."

The three girls split up a couple of blocks before the school, with Honey and Norma heading downtown. Trixie hurried on, with Reddy bounding along at her side. "Bobby will be so happy to see you," she told the Irish setter. She felt a slight twinge as she realized that she'd miss the reunion. *But I'll be there to give the good news to David Llewelyn*, she thought. *That will be just as exciting.*

At school, she tied Reddy's leash to the door handle of the Bob-Whites' station wagon, then ran into the building to find the boys.

She found Brian and Jim just finishing up at

the sign-up table. "You've got to come with me," she said. "Right now. One of you, at least."

Brian and Jim looked at her, then at one another. Then Jim put the money they'd just collected into his shirt pocket, while Brian grabbed the coats that were lying on the floor.

Seeing that they were about to follow, Trixie headed back to the parking lot. Reddy was still tied to the station wagon, but when he saw Trixie, he broke loose and ran toward her. Then, seeing Jim and Brian come out of the building, he ran past her to give the boys an enthusiastic greeting.

"Where'd you find him?" Brian asked. It was clear that he was too happy to really care about the answer. Jim, however, gave Trixie another close look.

"He just kind of—uh—turned up," she said lamely.

"So," Brian said, "your suspicion turned out to be without foundation."

"Foundation?" Trixie started guiltily, thinking for a moment that Brian had somehow guessed at her suspicions of Paul Gale and his phony foundation. Then she realized she'd misunderstood. "Oh. No. The foundation

wasn't—I mean, there was no foundation behind the sabotage. None at all."

Jim's gaze had become more and more suspicious. Trixie felt that she had to get away
immediately or risk being trapped. *I can't
take the time to explain everything that's happened,* she thought. *It would take too long,
and then I'd never catch up to Honey and
Norma.*

"Well, listen," she said out loud, "I just doubled back here to drop the dog off. Now I have
to meet Honey. She's downtown, working on
something. It's a surprise so I can't tell you
much about it, except that it's connected with
the pet show." *Which is true,* she thought,
*since it was the pet show sabotage that led us
to Paul Gale and David Llewelyn.* "We'll catch
the second bus home," she added. "Don't
bother to wait for us."

She turned and walked as decorously as she
could away from the school. It was only when
she was out of sight that she began to run. The
cold air hurt her lungs, but she was too eager
to find Honey and Norma to stop running.

There was no sign of the two girls, or of
David Llewelyn, anywhere on the block in
front of the World Anti-Hunger Foundation.

On a hunch, Trixie headed for the cafe. There she found the three people she was looking for.

Norma had just finished transferring her information to David Llewelyn. "The woman laughed after Paul Gale made the remark about ice," Norma was concluding. "Then she came out of the back room. She seemed surprised to see me. When I told her I wanted to talk to Paul Gale, she told me he wasn't in and that I'd better come back some other time. So I left."

"That proves it, doesn't it?" Trixie asked excitedly.

"It's proof enough for me," David Llewelyn said.

"Isn't it proof enough for a judge?" Trixie asked.

David Llewelyn shook his head. "Not all by itself."

Norma looked disappointed. "I didn't really help, then, did I?"

"Why don't you wire her?" Trixie suggested. "It didn't work when I tried it, because I was hoping to get him to confess to something he hadn't done. But Norma could use his own words against him. That would be a lot more effective."

"It would also be a lot more dangerous," the investigator said.

"If I do it, is there a chance I'd get real evidence against Paul Gale?" Norma asked.

"There's a chance," David Llewelyn told her.

"Then I'll do it," she said.

Trixie looked admiringly at Norma. *She has a lot of courage. I guess she's shown that all along, going out in the cold every day, but this is different.*

"Would you like us to go with you, Norma?" Honey asked.

"Oh, would you?" the girl responded eagerly.

"Of course, we would," Trixie said.

David Llewelyn took the microphone from his pocket. There was no place to conceal it on Norma's open-necked blouse and vest, so he clipped it to the hood of her parka, where the fur concealed it. He explained again that he would be taping the conversation. "Keep him talking until you're absolutely sure you've got the evidence," he said. "If we move in too soon, we'll probably lose him for good."

Norma nodded solemnly.

"Remember, don't put yourselves in any danger," he said. "I'd rather lose Paul Gale than lose you. Understand?"

Norma gulped and nodded.

David Llewelyn and the three girls left the booth and walked outside. The investigator faded from sight, while Trixie, Honey, and Norma headed for the foundation office.

The assistant was once again alone in the main room.

"I'd like to talk to Paul Gale," Norma said.

"He isn't here," the woman said curtly.

"Not even in the back room?" Norma asked. "This is important. It's about birdseed." She made the last statement in a voice loud enough to carry through the closed door to the back room.

Paul Gale's assistant looked shaken. "I'll, uh, see if he's available," she said.

She disappeared through the door. The girls heard a rumble of low conversation, but they couldn't pick out any of the words. In less than a minute, the assistant was back. "Mr. Gale will see you," she said, holding the door open for them.

The back room was comfortable but not lavish. There was a large desk with a swivel chair, a couch, and an armchair, as well as a file cabinet and a messy bookcase. Paul Gale rose from the swivel chair as the girls entered the room. "Why don't you take off your coats and make yourselves comfortable?" he said, gesturing toward the couch and easy chair.

Norma shot a nervous look at Trixie and Honey. The last thing they wanted was for Norma to take off her coat, with its concealed microphone.

"Oh, come now," Paul Gale said. "You have to take off your coats. Otherwise you'll catch cold when you go back outside."

*There's no choice,* Trixie thought. *We either take off our coats and sit down, or refuse to take them off and leave. As long as the coats are in the room, the microphone will probably still pick up the conversation.* She unzipped her jacket and threw it casually over the arm of the chair.

Norma and Honey quickly followed her example. Then the assistant appeared again. She scooped up the coats and took them back to the front room, closing the door behind her as she went.

*Oh, no!* Trixie thought. *Now Mr. Llewelyn won't be able to tape the conversation at all. Well, there are three of us to testify to what we hear, so maybe the tape won't be that impor-*

*tant. I just hope Mr. Llewelyn doesn't panic
and come in after us.*

"Now," Paul Gale said, "what was it you
wanted?"

"I-I wanted to talk to you," Norma said. "I
wanted to find out more about the ice you
bring back from the Far East."

Paul Gale smiled slyly. "I don't know what
you're talking about. Do you mean rice? Some
of the Far Eastern countries do export rice, although they should be keeping it to feed their
own people."

"Ice," Trixie corrected him. There was no
time for subtlety. They had to get the evidence
before David Llewelyn came to get them.
"Ice, as in gems bought with money that's supposed to buy food for the poor."

Paul Gale's smile faded gradually as he realized that there was indeed no misunderstanding. "Who put you onto me?" he demanded.

"I figured it out for myself," Norma said
smugly.

Paul Gale paused to plan his next move.
"You're right," he admitted. "I do use foundation money to buy gems.

"It didn't start out that way, you understand.
At first, all of the money really did go to buy

food. Then, on one trip, someone offered me a huge, perfect ruby. The price was ridiculously low. I thought I could bring it back to this country, sell it, and have that much more money to use for food. Once I had the money, though, it seemed fair for me to keep a little part of it, as long as I gave the rest to the foundation. It was nice to have some money of my own, after all those years of giving everything away."

Paul Gale wasn't looking at the girls as he talked. He was staring at the wall, but seeming to look back into the past. "On the next trip, the same man offered me two rubies to bring back here. He wanted twice as much money, of course. I thought about using my own money. In the end, though, I used money from the foundation. This time, I didn't put any of it back.

"That's how it started. From there it just grew. It was like a game that I couldn't stop playing. I don't even sell the gems anymore. I don't need the money. I just keep them, look at them. They're beautiful. Have you ever seen a really big beautiful ruby or diamond?" He suddenly turned a direct gaze at the girls.

The girls shook their heads.

"Would you like to? I have some out back in my camper. I'll even give you some, if you'll promise to go away and leave me alone."

Trixie felt a burst of anger at Paul Gale's offer of a bribe. Then she quickly turned the offer to her advantage. *If we actually get to see the gems, we'll have an ironclad case against him,* she thought.

"It's a deal," Norma said.

*She must be thinking the same thing.* A barely perceptible nod from Honey told Trixie that all three girls were in tune.

Paul Gale stood up. "Come on, then. The camper is right out back, so you don't need your coats."

He held open the back door. Through it, Trixie could see a green pickup truck with a white camper top. Paul Gale opened the door of the camper, and the girls hurried to jump inside, out of the cold wind.

It was dark in the camper. Trixie turned and saw Paul Gale's thin frame outlined in the light of the open door. "You want to see gems?" he said tauntingly. "Well, they're in there somewhere. And I'll give you all the time in the world to find them. All the time you have left in the world, anyway." He took a step backward and slammed the door.

The inside of the camper went almost black. Trixie lunged for the door. "It's locked!" she exclaimed.

"The windows don't open, either!" Honey cried.

Suddenly the girls began to be aware of the cold. The icy air quickly penetrated their clothes.

"He's left us out here to freeze to death," Norma said in a low voice.

Trixie tried to sound hopeful. "Someone will come along and find us," she said. Then the door of the pickup slammed shut, and someone started the engine. *What now?* Trixie thought frantically.

The truck lurched through the alley and out onto the street. Trixie tried to keep track of their path, noting all the turns. But her quiet concentration only made her aware of how cold she was getting. "Stomp your feet and clap your hands together," she told the other girls.

"It hurts," Norma said after a couple of stomps.

"You'd be a lot worse off if it didn't," Trixie told her.

That warning was enough to keep the girls interested in exercise for a few moments. But their attention was distracted when the truck rolled to a stop. The engine was turned off, and the door of the truck opened and closed. Another engine was still running somewhere nearby, however. In the distance a car door slammed. Then the car drove away, and all was still.

Fear settled around the girls like a blanket, but there was no warmth in it. "Let's keep moving," Trixie said. She flapped her arms up and down and made scissors motions with her legs. Honey and Norma did the same.

Eventually, however, Trixie couldn't move anymore. Her muscles ached from the exercise almost as much as her fingers and toes ached from the cold.

"I can't take it anymore," Honey said, echoing Trixie's thoughts.

"I'm getting sleepy," Norma said with a yawn in her voice.

"Don't go to sleep," Trixie said. "That's how people freeze to death. We have to keep talking."

"What should we talk about?" Honey asked.

"Summer," Trixie said. "Think about warm

sun, and riding our bikes, and cookouts by the pond." She felt a lump in her throat. *Making myself sad is no help at all*, she thought.

"Let's think about adventure," Honey said. "That should keep our blood racing. Remember when we went off in the red trailer to find my brother Jim?"

Trixie remembered happily, and she and Honey took turns telling the story to Norma. When they ended, however, there was no response from their listener.

"Norma?" Trixie said.

"Mmm—sleepy," came the drowsy reply.

Trixie heard Honey yawn, and it triggered her own yawning reflex. "We can't . . . we can't fall asleep . . ." Trixie murmured. As she spoke, she did seem to be falling—falling through space to somewhere dark and warm.

She began to dream. It was morning, and she was in her bed at home. She must have been very young in the dream, she realized, because someone was washing her face, the way she still sometimes washed Bobby's. She must have gotten very dirty somehow, because someone seemed to be angry with her, and saying her name loudly, over and over: "Trixie, Trixie, Trixie." All the while, the rough washcloth was scrubbing her face.

Trixie struggled to open her eyes. She expected to see the familiar walls of her bedroom, but she didn't. She expected to see her mother's face, but she didn't see that, either. Instead, she saw—

"Reddy!" Trixie shouted. She pushed the dog away as he continued to try to lick her face. She sat up and looked around. The door of the camper was open, and dim late-afternoon light was streaming in. She could see Honey groggily sitting up at her brother Jim's urging. Brian Belden was patting Norma's cold hands, trying to bring her around.

Someone was standing in the doorway. Trixie stifled a scream, remembering her last sight of Paul Gale. The voice that spoke, though, was the calm one of David Llewelyn. "I'm glad to see that you're all right," he said, "although it's certainly no credit to me that you are."

# 14 * Success!

TRIXIE WAS only dimly aware of being helped out of the camper and into a waiting car. Much later, it seemed, she was lifted out of the car again. This time, she did wind up back in her own bedroom.

When she woke again, it was full daylight. She opened her eyes to see Bobby's worried face close to hers.

"She's awake!" he shouted without moving away. "Trixie's awake! You're awake, aren't you, Trixie?"

Trixie squeezed her eyes shut against the noise. "I'm awake."

"I was just waiting for you to wake up because I wanted to tell you thanks for finding Reddy," Bobby said.

"Actually, it's Trixie who should thank Reddy for finding her," Brian Belden said from the doorway.

Trixie looked up at her brother just as Mart joined him. "What happened?" she asked.

"Well, first of all," Brian said, coming into the room and sitting down, "Jim was suspicious about that little errand of yours. Something you said about a foundation struck him funny. He suggested we stop by the foundation office on the way home. When we got there, the lights were on, but the door was locked."

"Paul Gale's assistant must have locked up so she could follow us and pick him up after he got out of the truck," Trixie said.

"Probably," Brian agreed. "We didn't know that, though, so we were about to give up and take off. That's when Reddy came to the rescue. He got away from us and ran into that alley between the buildings. We chased him to the back of the alley, just in time to see Paul Gale's green pickup truck and the maroon sedan the assistant was driving as they pulled away.

"We didn't think much about the vehicles at the time, in spite of the fuss Reddy was making. But when we got back to the sidewalk, Mr. Llewelyn was there. He'd gotten nervous when he saw that the front door was locked.

"We exchanged information. Mr. Llewelyn told us about the microphone. He'd heard Paul Gale ask you to take off your coats, so he didn't expect to pick up any conversation. He'd decided to give you some time before going in after you. Then we figured out that you girls were in the camper."

"It took you long enough to find us," Trixie said, still a little shaken.

"It would have been a whole lot longer without a good description of the vehicle," Brian said. "That was a close call, Trix."

Trixie shuddered. "Are Honey and Norma okay?"

"They're fine," Brian assured her.

Suddenly drowsy again, Trixie smiled as she drifted back to sleep. "Just think," she murmured, "it was Reddy to the rescue."

By Saturday morning, Trixie was fully re-
covered. As the Beldens gathered for an early
breakfast, it was Mart who seemed to be under
the weather.

"I was up until midnight last night, input-
ting the last of the data. Now I have to bolt my
breakfast and return to the computer room to
run the program. After that, no more programs
for me!"

"I thought computerizing the categories
was going to be a big labor-saver," Trixie reminded him.

"It was," Mart said. "Unfortunately, though,
the labor that was saved was yours; the labor
that was expended was exclusively my own."

"By the way," said Brian, "is there any news
about Paul Gale?"

Trixie frowned. "No. I've left messages for
David Llewelyn every day, but he hasn't returned them. I hope Paul Gale doesn't get
away to start some other con game in another
town."

"An awful thought," Mart said. "Speaking of
getaways, Brian and I must make one. Are you
ready, my faithful charioteer?"

"Ready," Brian mumbled through his last mouthful of pancakes. "I'll sure be glad when you get a senior driver's license!"

"See you at the show," Trixie said. "I can hardly wait to see the categories."

Less than two hours later, all of the show volunteers but Mart were in the gym. The judging table was set up in the center of the room. Other tables were lined up against the walls, ready for cages and carriers.

"Now all we need are the pets," Trixie said, surveying their work with satisfaction.

"Which pets are those?" Mart asked, striding across the room, holding a sheaf of computer paper. "The heaviest pet—Clancy the sheepdog at ninety-one pounds? The lightest pet—Percy the parakeet at two ounces? The most intelligent pet—Samantha the Siamese cat?"

"Yay! The program worked!" Trixie said.

"Naturally," Mart said proudly.

"What other categories are there?" Di asked as she crowded around, along with the other Bob-Whites.

Mart turned the printout paper around so that he could read it. "Oldest. Youngest. Most unusual—that's a cockatiel. Longest ears—"

"A rabbit?" Trixie guessed.

"A basset hound," Mart corrected. "I had to give the rabbit 'shortest tail' to make up for Barney's infringement on Mopsy's natural category."

"And you really have a category for each and every animal!" Di exclaimed admiringly.

"It's going to be fun to be surrounded by so many animals today," Norma Nelson said. "I really appreciate your letting me help with the pet show."

"It was the least we could do, after you helped us solve the mystery," Trixie said.

"The Paul Gale mystery," Brian added. "You know, you girls never did solve the mystery of the pet show sabotage."

Norma started to turn red, and Trixie felt her own cheeks growing hot. *The other Bob-Whites still didn't know about Norma*, Trixie thought. *We'll have to tell them; it's not right for the Bob-Whites to have secrets from one another. It's not right for people like Norma and Gordon to be jealous of us, either. That's something we'll all have to work on together. But the pet show comes first. We can't let anything—not even the solution to the mystery—distract us from that.*

As usual, Honey's tact came to the rescue. "You said yourself that there was no harm done, Brian. What does it matter if we ever catch the culprit?"

"Ah, but we have."

The Bob-Whites and Norma Nelson turned to see David Llewelyn approaching. "I take it you're talking about Paul Gale," he said. "We tracked him down, finally. It took three long days, but he and his assistant are safely behind bars."

"We weren't talking about Paul Gale, actually, but that's certainly good news," Trixie said. Seeing David Llewelyn's tired face, she forgave him immediately for not returning her messages. *I'll bet he hasn't slept since he pulled us out of that camper*, she thought.

"I'll be returning home now for a good long rest," David Llewelyn continued. "I just dropped by to clear up the matter of the reward."

"Reward?" Trixie said.

"One thousand dollars for information leading to the arrest of perpetrators of large-scale consumer crime," David Llewelyn said. "Would you three girls like to divide it equally?"

"Oh, no," Trixie said. "It's Norma's money; she was the one who produced the evidence."

"That's right," Honey said.

Everyone turned to look at Norma. She just stood staring back at them, speechless.

"That will buy a lot of birdseed," David Llewelyn said.

Then Norma's face brightened. "Oh, it would! Could I really use it for that?" she asked, looking at Trixie and Honey.

"It's your money," Trixie told her.

Norma hesitated. "I think we should give half the money to a *real* anti-hunger foundation."

"That would be wonderful," Honey agreed.

"It would," Trixie said. "In fact, for the next Bob-White fund-raiser we could—"

Trixie was interrupted by the arrival of the first entrants in the show. They were followed by a trickle and then a steady stream of additional entrants. Soon everyone was settled and ready to begin.

"It's all up to Dr. Chang and the animals, now," Trixie said as she, Honey, and Norma took their places in the bleachers.

Dr. Chang and the animals were a winning combination. One at a time, Dr. Chang put the animals on display on or in front of the judging table. Trixie was amazed at how much he knew about the different species. He had a specific comment to make on nearly every entrant; that the shape of its head was good, or that the color of its eyes was exceptional, or that it was unusually large or small for its breed.

A steady sound of ooh's and aah's at the adorable animals was mixed with laughter at their antics. One of the merriest responses was, predictably, to Reddy and Bobby Belden. When his name was called, the six-year-old started toward the center of the gym with all the dignity he could muster—while his dog started off in the other direction. Since the dog was larger than the boy, Reddy's choice of direction won out, and Bobby was pulled along behind.

Only prolonged calling and whistling from Dr. Chang drew Reddy to the judging table.

"Oh, woe," Trixie moaned, sinking down as far as she could on the bleacher seat. "Why did we let Bobby enter Reddy in this contest?"

"He's adorable," Honey retorted, "and you know it."

"He really is," Norma agreed. "He's very intelligent, too. Why, with a few weeks of obedience training, I bet he'd be a champion."

Trixie and Honey stared at her blankly for a moment. Then they burst into peals of laughter.

Norma turned bright red. "Oh—you meant Bobby." She lowered her head and stared at her feet.

Desperately, Trixie tried to stop laughing. *She's bound to think we're making fun of her. How is she supposed to know that sending Bobby to obedience school is so logical it's funny?*

Then Norma's shoulders began to shake slightly. A small squeaky noise came from her throat. The squeak became a giggle and then, finally, full-scale laughter.

Norma's laughter set Trixie and Honey off again, too. Soon all three girls were rocking back and forth on the bleachers, holding their sides.

Their laughter was only beginning to subside when Dr. Chang finished his examination of Reddy and instructed Bobby to take the dog back to his place against the wall. The sight of the boy and his dog taking off, once again, in different directions, renewed their laughter. By now, however, the entire crowd was roaring, so the girls didn't have to worry about being conspicuous.

Shortly after Reddy's turn, Dr. Chang finished judging the other pets. Then he called a brief intermission, inviting the audience to vote for the People's Choice Award while he made his decisions.

Mr. and Mrs. Belden and Miss Trask made their way through the crowd to compliment the Bob-Whites on their success.

"Just think," Trixie said with a sigh after they'd left, "in a few minutes, it will all be over."

"Yes," Mart said with a sigh that mocked his sister's. "Won't it be sad? No more tearing my hair out over my nonworking computer program. No more listening to your bizarre theories about someone sabotaging the pet show. No more—"

"No more!" Trixie said hurriedly. She glanced at Norma.

"Actually, there's lots more," said Brian. "We gathered over two hundred dollars during the entry phase of the show. We probably doubled that with our ticket sales today. That will buy a lot of cracked corn, which will mean a lot of game-bird feeding over the next few weeks."

Further conversation was interrupted by Dr. Chang's call for the crowd to take their places.

"This was a difficult show to judge," he said, "because every animal here is exceptional. I hope that I've reached decisions that you consider to be fair."

With that short speech, he began to hand out the awards. For the most part, he followed Mart's printout list. Largest, smallest, longest ears, shortest tail, furriest, *un*furriest—one by one, Dr. Chang awarded each animal a bright purple ribbon. The crowd cheered them all, and they all—owners and pets alike—looked proud and happy.

The Bob-Whites, and Norma, cheered especially loudly when Dr. Chang announced the prize for the People's Choice Award. Reddy won it, of course!

When the contest was over and the crowd began filing out of the gym, Bobby rushed over to his sister. Reddy bounded along beside him.

Bobby held up his trophy for Trixie to see. "We won!" he crowed. "We won at the pet show!"

"Of course," Trixie said, kneeling down to hug him. She looked at Norma Nelson and at her fellow Bob-Whites. "Didn't you know? In this show, everyone was a winner!"